EROTICON 2

'I presume,' began the Monsignor, 'your friend will not be shocked if we initiate him into the mysteries our priestly employment permits us to enjoy. Eh, Boniface?'

'I expect, Monsignor, that Mr Clinton knows just as much about birching as we do ourselves.'

At the first keen swish poor Lucy shrieked out, but before half a dozen had descended her groans subsided and she spoke in a quick, strained voice, begging for mercy.

'For the love of God,' she said, 'do not lay it on so strong.' Large bands of velvet, securely buckled at the sides, held her in position, while her legs, brought together and fastened in the same way, slightly elevated her soft, shapely arse.

'Oh!' cried Lucy, 'I feel so funny. Oh! Mr Clinton, if you are there, pray relieve me, and make haste!'

A NEXUS CLASSIC

EROTICON 2

Introduced and edited by J-P Spencer

This book is a work of fiction.
In real life, make sure you practise safe sex.

First published in 1986 by
Nexus
Thames Wharf Studios
Rainville Road
London W6 9HA

This Nexus Classic edition 2001

Introduction copyright © J-P Spencer 1986

www.nexus-books.co.uk

Typeset by TW Typesetting, Plymouth, Devon

Printed and bound by Omnia Books

ISBN 0 352 33594 7

Contents

INTRODUCTION

We can put names to very few of the authors responsible for the excerpts in this anthology of erotic writing. Ironically, those that are attributable are the most venerable in the collection. It is as if age, as in other spheres of activity, has lent respectability and, unlike their later counterparts, the old pornographers are content to stand up and be counted.

The Lascivious Monk, also known as *The Story of Dom B. . .*, first appeared in Paris at the beginning of 1741. It is a thoroughly entertaining and skilful sexual satire aimed squarely at the Church, and its success launched an entire genre of similar works. Its cheerful obscenity and anti-clerical content created a furore on publication. As proof of its subversive nature, the authorities launched an investigation which lasted four months and, apart from small fry such as printers and booksellers, pointed the finger at a nobleman and, appropriately, a priest. The real author however, Jean-Charles Gervaise de Latouche, was never brought to account. After the fuss surrounding the publication had subsided, he resumed his career as a lawyer and practised at the Parlement de Paris. Born in Amiens in 1715, he died in 1782, reputedly of grief following the bankruptcy of a nobleman to whom he had made over all his property in return for a life annuity.

A great deal could, and indeed has been, said about the author of *My Conversion* or *The Libertine of Quality*. Honoré Gabriel Riqueti, Comte de Mirabeau

(1749–91) was a libertine of repute himself, who emerged as the greatest orator of the French Revolution and died a hero of the people. *My Conversion* was written during one of his many periods of incarceration invoked by his tyrannical father under the iniquitous system of *lettres de cachet*. At the time, in early 1780, Mirabeau had been imprisoned in the Chateau of Vincennes for nearly three years, he was separated from his beloved mistress and their child (whom he had never seen) and, despite his many talents, his life to date had been one of frustration and rejection. As a consequence, the book is as much an act of revenge on the establishment which had turned its back on him, as a work of titillation. *My Conversion* was first published in 1783 and, notwithstanding frequent persecution by the authorities, it has survived many editions.

Andrea de Nercia (1739–1800), the author of *The Pleasures of Lolotte* or *Mon Noviciat*, is a similarly larger than life character from eighteenth-century France. The son of a Dijon lawyer, his career took many turns; he was, variously, a linguist, soldier, playwright, novelist, composer, librarian and spy. This last activity had him dogging the footsteps of Madame Buonaparte in Italy in 1797. Queen Marie-Caroline subsequently sent him on a secret mission to the Pope with the result that he was imprisoned in the Castel Sant' Angelo in Rome. Though released at the turn of the century, his health was broken and he died in Naples in 1800. *The Pleasures of Lolotte* — in which the anti-clerical influence of previous works such as *The Lascivious Monk* and *My Conversion* can plainly be seen—was first published in Berlin in 1792.

The other selections included here encompass a

wide variety of erotic writing, from the Victorian naughtiness of *A Man with a Maid*, which manages to be coy, silly and rude in equal degress, to a pastiche of Cleland's *Memoirs of a Woman of Pleasure* in *Fanny Hill's Daughter*, to *Maudie*, an item of Edwardian froth, enlivened by a bevy of flappers and some ripping period slang.

As in the first anthology in this series, further extracts have been taken from *Pauline the Prima Donna*, also known as *The Memoirs of a German Singer*, the (fictional) autobiography of the celebrated diva Wilhelmina Schroeder-Devrient (1804–60); *The House of Borgia*, by the pseudonymous Marcus Van Heller, a stalwart of the Olympia Press stable in the mid-1950s; and 'Walter's' notorious sexual diary, *My Secret Life*. This last is doubtless the most extraordinary account yet written of one man's amatory experiences. Published in a very limited edition *circa* 1890, it runs to eleven volumes. By no means all of this material is widely available and the selection printed here is from the less readily accessible portion. Much has been written about this unique book and all commentators are agreed that the events recounted represent the truth as the author saw it at the time. This can make for some bizarre reading as, for example, in the extract quoted here in which the ever-prurient Walter peeps at a man with a formidable penis:

Going to a round small mahogany table and taking the cloth off it, he thwacked and banged his prick on it, and a sound came as if the table had been hit with a stick — 'It does not hurt me,' he said.—I was never so astonished in my life.

Readers interested in learning more about this obsessive but fascinating work—and erotic writing in general—are recommended to turn to Gordon Grimley's edition of *My Secret Life* (Panther), Steven Marcus's *The Other Victorians* (Weidenfeld & Nicolson/ Corgi) and Patrick J Kearney's *A History of Erotic Literature*.

This volume is only a sampler intended to provide an introduction to a little known world. The literature of sexual imagination is a long and curious highway which follows many intriguing twists and turns. *Erotican II* invites the interested reader to survey just a few of the secret and mysterious landmarks along its fabulous route.

J-P Spencer

The Lascivious Monk

Translated from the French by Howard Nelson

Slowly we walked, not in the tree-lined paths but among the open garden beds where the rays of the sun were the hottest. The only protection Madame Dinville had was a little fan. I had nothing, but I suffered my tortures stoically. The Abbot was laughing at our foolishness, but he soon became discouraged after we went around several times. I still could not guess what Madame Dinville had in mind. Also, I could not understand how she was able to stand the burning heat which I was beginning to find unbearable. Little did I realize that rich reward I was to get for my faithful service.

Our stubbornness in continuing the walk soon bored the scoffing Abbot and he retired. When we were at the end of one of the paths, Madame Dinville led me into a pleasantly cool little arbor.

'Aren't we going to go on with our stroll?' I innocently asked.

'No, I think I've had enough sun,' she replied.

She regarded me searchingly to learn if I guessed the reason for the promenade, and she perceived that I had no idea of the blessing she was intending for me. She took my arms which she squeezed affectionately. Then, as if she were extremely tired, she rested her head on my shoulder and put her face so close to mine that I would have been a fool not to kiss. She made no objection.

'Oh, oh,' I thought to myself. 'So that's her game. Well, nobody will disturb us here.'

12

In truth, we were in a sort of labyrinth whose obscurity and turnings and windings would conceal us from the sharpest eyes.

Now she sat down under a bower on the grass. It was the ideal setting for the purpose I was sure she had in mind. Following her example, I seated myself at her side. She gave me a soulful look, squeezed my hand, and reclined on her back. Believing that the moment had come, I started to ready my weapon when all of a sudden she fell sound asleep. At first, I thought it was only drowsiness caused by the heat and that I could easily rouse her. But when she refused to wake up after repeated shakings, I was simple enough to believe in the genuineness of a slumber that I should have suspected because of its promptness and profundity.

'My usual luck,' I swore to myself. 'If she fell asleep after I had quenched my desires, I wouldn't mind, but to be so cruel at the moment when she had raised my hopes so high is unpardonable.'

I was inconsolable. There was sadness in my heart as I regarded her. She was dressed like the previous day, that is to say, with the diaphanous blouse which revealed her unbelievable breasts, that were so near and yet so far. As the strawberry-tipped orbs rose and fell, I longingly admired their whiteness and symmetry.

My desires were almost at the breaking point, and I felt the urge to wake her up, but I dismissed the desire for fear that she would get angry. She would have to awaken eventually, I reflected, but I could not resist the urge to put my hand on that seductive bosom.

'She is sleeping too soundly for her to awaken at

my touch,' I said to myself, 'but if she does, the worst that she can do is scold me for my boldness.'

Extending a quivering hand to one of the inviting mounds, I kept an anxious eye on her face, ready to retreat at the first sign of life. But she slumbered peacefully on as I lifted her blouse up to her neck and let my fingers graze the satin-smooth contours. My hand was like a swallow skimming over the water, now and then dipping its wings in the waves.

Now I was emboldened to plant a tender kiss on one rose-bud. She still did not stir. Then the other was given the same treatment. Changing my position, I became even naughtier. I put my head under her skirt in order to penetrate into the obscure landscape of love, but I could not make out anything for her legs were crossed. If I could not see it, at least I was going to touch it. My hand slowly crept up the thigh until it reached the foot of the Venusberg. The tip of my finger was already at the entrance to the grotto. I had gone too far, I decided, but having reached this point, I was more miserable and frustrated than ever. I was so anxious to see what I was touching. With-drawing the intruding hand, I sat up again and regarded the visage of my sleeping beauty. There was no change in her placid expression. It seemed that Morpheus had cast his most soporific poppies on her.

Did my eyes deceive me? Did one of her eyelids twitch? I felt a sense of near panic. I looked again, this time more closely. No, the eye I thought had momentarily opened was still tightly shut.

Reassured, I took new courage and began to gently lift up her skirt. She gave a slight start, and I was positive that I had awakened her. Quickly, I pulled the skirt back down. My heart was pounding as if I had narrowly escaped a disaster. I was terror-stricken as I sat again at her side and feasted my eyes on her admirable bosom. With relief, I saw that there was not a sign of returning life. She had just changed position, and what a delightful new position it was.

Her thighs were now uncrossed. When she raised one knee, the skirt fell on her stomach, revealing her hirsute mound and cunt. The dazzling sight almost intoxicated me. Picture to yourself a rounded leg encased in a frivolous stocking held up by a dainty garter, a tiny foot in a saucy shoe, and thighs of alabaster. The carmine red cunt was surrounded by a ring of ebony black hair and it exuded a scent more heady than the rarest incense. Inserting my finger in the aperture, I tickled it a little. At this, she opened her legs still wider. Then I put my mouth to it, trying to sink my tongue to the very bottom. Words cannot describe the straining erection I had.

Nothing could stop me now. Fear, respect and caution were thrown to the winds. My passion was like a torrent, seeping away everything in its path. If she had been the Sultan's favourite, I would have fucked her in the presence of a hundred eunuchs armed with sharp scimitars. Stretching my body over her and supporting myself with my hands and knees so that my weight would not arouse her, my member gradually disappeared into the hole. The only part of me touching her was my prick which I gently pushed in and pulled out. The slow but regular cadence enhanced and prolonged my ineffable bliss.

Still carefully watching her face, I gently kissed her full lips from time to time.

But the raptures I was experiencing were so great

that I forgot my caution and fell heavily on the lady, furiously hugging and embracing her.

The climax of my pleasure opened my eyes which had been shut since I had entered her, and I saw the transports of Madame Dinville, joys which I was no longer able to share. My somnolent friend had just clutched my buttocks with her hands, and raising hers which she convulsively wiggled, she dragged me down hard on her quivering body. I kissed her with the last of the passion I had left.

'My dear friend,' she moaned in a failing voice, 'push a little more. Don't leave me half way to my goal.'

I felt renewed vigour at her touching appeal and resumed my enjoyable task. After barely five or six strokes more, she really lost consciousness. For some unknown reason, that excited me and I quickened my tempo. In a matter of seconds, I reached the peak again and fell into a state like that of my partner. When we revived, we showed our appreciation of each other with warm kisses and tight embraces.

With the fading of passion, I felt I had to withdraw, but I was embarrassed for I was unwilling for her to see the sorry condition my prick was in. I tried to hide it, but her eyes were fixed on me. When it was out, she grabbed it, took it into her mouth, and began to suck it.

'What were you trying to do, you silly boy?' she murmured. 'Were you ashamed to show me an instrument you know how to use so well? Did I conceal anything from you? Look! Here are my breasts. Look at them and fondle them as much as you want. Take those rosy tips in your mouth and put your hand on my cunt. Oh, that's wonderful! You have no idea of the pleasure you're giving me, you little rascal.'

Animated by the vivacity of her caresses, I responded with equal ardour. She marvelled at the dexterity of my finger as she rolled her eyes and breathed her sighs into my mouth.

My prick, having regained its pristine rigidity from her lips on it, wanted her more than ever. Before putting it in her again, I spread open her thighs to feast my eyes on that seat of delight. Often these preliminaries to pleasure are more piquant than pleasure itself. Is there anything more exquisite than to have a woman willing to assume any position your lascivious imagination can conjure? I experienced an ecstatic vertigo as I put my nose to that adorable cunt. I wished that all of me were a prick so that I could be completely engulfed in it. Desire begat even more violent desires.

Reveal a portion of your bosom to your lover, and he insists on seeing it all. Show him a little firm white breast, and he clamours to touch it. He is a dipsomaniac whose thirst increases as he drinks. Let him touch, and he demands to kiss it. Permit him to wander farther down, he commands that you let him put his prick there. His ingenious mind comes up with the most capricious fantasies, and he is not satisfied until he can carry them out on you.

The reader can imagine how long I was content nuzzling that appetizing aperture. It was a matter of seconds until I was again vigorously fucking her. She eagerly responded with upward thrusts to match my powerful lunges. In order to get farther in, I had my hands on the cheeks of her derriere while she had her legs wrapped around my back. Our mouths, glued to each other, were two cunts being mutually fucked by two tongues. Finally came the ecstasy that lifted us to the heights and then annihilated us.

It has been said that potency is a gift of the gods, and although they had been more than generous with me, I was squandering my divine patrimony, and I had need of every drop of the heavenly largesse to emerge from the present engagement with honour.

It seemed that her desires were increasing in proportion to the loss of my powers. Only with the most libertine caresses was she able to turn my imminent retreat into still another victory. This she accomplished by getting on top of me, letting her full breasts dangle above my face and rubbing my failing virility with her cunt which seemed possessed of a life of its own.

'Now, I'm fucking you!' she joyously cried as she bounced up and down on me. Motionless, I let her do what she wanted with me. It was a delightful sensation, the first one I had ever enjoyed in that way. Now and then, she paused in her exertions to rain kisses on my face. Those lovely orbs swayed rhythmically above me in time with her repeated impaling of herself. When they came close to my mouth, I eagerly kissed or sucked the rose nipple. A streak of voluptuousness shuddering through my body announced the imminence of the supreme moment. Joining my transports to hers, I gushed just at the moment she did, and our juices mingled with the perspiration on our bellies.

Exhausted and shattered by the assaults I had launched and withstood for more than two hours, I felt an overwhelming desire for sleep and I yielded to it. Madame Dinville herself rested my head on her abundant bosom, wanting also to enjoy some rest, but with me in her arms.

'Sleep, my love,' she murmured as she wiped the perspiration from my forehead. 'Have a good sleep, for I know how much you need it.'

I dozed off immediately, only to awaken when the sun was sinking on the horizon. The first thing I saw when I opened my eyes was Madame Dinville. She looked at me cheerfully, interrupting the knitting she had occupied herself with during my slumber to dart her tongue in my mouth.

She made no attempt to conceal her desire for a resumption of the sport, but I had little interest. My indifference irritated her. It was not that I was disinclined, but if it had been left up to me, I would have preferred repose to action. But Madame was not going to have it that way. Holding me in her arms, she overwhelmed me with proofs of her passion, but they did not arouse me, even though I tried my best to stroke the dead fires within me.

Disappointed at her lack of success, she employed another ruse to relight my extinguished flames. Lying on her back, she raised her skirt to her navel, revealing the object of the desires of most men. She well knew the effect such an exposure would produce. When she suggestively jiggled her buttocks, I felt something stirring in me and I placed my hand on the gift she was offering me. But it was only a token gesture of passion. As I was negligently titillating her clitoris, she was feverishly massaging my prick in a hysterical cadence dictated by her feverish eagerness. When my prick finally stood up, I saw her eyes sparkle in triumph at her success in reviving my ardour. Now aroused by her caresses, I promptly bestowed on her

19

the tokens of my gratitude which she zealously accepted. Grasping me around the waist, she bumped up and down under me so violently that I ejaculated almost automatically, but with such raptures that I was angry with myself for having ended the joy so promptly.

Now it was time to leave the arbor which had been the scene of such transports. But before returning to the chateau, we took several turns in the labyrinth to allow the traces of our exertions to disappear. As we were strolling, we naturally chatted:

'How happy I am with you, dear Saturnin,' she remarked. 'Did I live up to your expectations?'

'I am still relishing the delights you were good enough to grant me,' I gallantly replied.

'Thank you,' she said. 'But it was not very wise of me to have surrendered to you the way I did. You will be discreet, won't you, Saturnin?'

I retorted that if she thought I was capable of betraying to others what joys we had, she must not have a very high opinion of me. She was so pleased with my astute response that she rewarded me with a long, lingering kiss. I am sure that I would have been rewarded much more richly had we not been in a spot where we could be seen. As an additional gratitude, she pressed my hand on her left breast with a meaningful expression.

Now we quickened our pace as the conversation languished. I noticed that Madame Dinville was anxiously looking from side to side and wondered why.

But who would have thought that after such an exhausting afternoon, she still wanted more? She wanted to crown the day with one last engagement, and she was on the lookout for some stray servant.

The reader will probably think that she had the devil in the flesh, and he would not be far off the mark.

She tried to revive me with her tongue and mouth, but the poor thing was lifeless. Sad but true. To attain her goal, what did she do? That is what we are going to find out.

As a youngster just getting to know the ways of the world, I flattered myself that I had made an auspicious debut and that I would be lacking in respect if I did not see her to her rooms. That done, I felt I could take my leave by giving her a final kiss for the day.

'What's that?' she demanded in a surprised tone. 'You're not leaving, are you? It's only eight o'clock. You stay here. I'll arrange things with your Cure.'

The thought of avoiding Mass appealed to me and I was agreeable to her interceding for me. Making me sit on the bed, she went to lock the door and returned to take her place at my side. She looked at me intently without uttering a word. Her silence disconcerted me.

'Don't you want to any more?' she finally said.

Because I knew I was finished, I was so embarrassed that I could not force out a word. To admit my impotence was unthinkable. I lowered my eyes to conceal my shame.

'We're all alone, dear Saturnin,' she said in a coaxing voice, bathing my face with hot kisses which just left me cold.

'Not a soul in the world can spy on us,' she continued. 'Let's take off our clothes and get into my bed. Come, my friend, down to the buff. I'll soon make the stubborn little prick stand up.'

Taking me in her arms, she actually carried me and deposited me on the couch where she disrobed me in a feverish impatience. She soon got me in the desired condition, that is to say, naked as the day I was born. More out of politeness than pleasure, I let her have her way with me.

Turning me on my back, she started sucking my poor prick. She had it in her mouth up to my testicles. I could see that she was in ecstasies as she covered the member with a saliva that resembled froth. She did restore some life to it, but so little that she could make no use of it. Recognizing that that treatment was of no avail, she went to her dressing-table and got a little flask containing a whitish fluid. This she poured on her palm and vigorously rubbed it on my balls and prick.

'There,' she said with satisfaction when she finished. 'You aren't through yet by any means.'

Impatiently I waited for the fulfilment of her prediction. Little tingles in my testicles raised my hopes for success. While waiting for the treatment to take effect, she undressed in turn. By the time she was naked, I felt as if my blood was boiling. My penis shot up as if released by a powerful spring. Like a maniac, I grabbed her and forced her on the bed with me. I devoured her, scarcely permitting her to breathe. I was blind and deaf. Sounds like those of an enraged beast came out of my mouth. There was only one thought in my mind, and that was her cunt.

'Stop, my love!' she cried, tearing herself from me. 'Not in such a hurry. Let's prolong our pleasures and elaborate on them. Put your head at my feet, and I'll do the same. Now your tongue in my cunt. That's it. Oh, I'm in heaven.'

My body, stretched out on her, was swimming in a sea of delight, I darted my tongue as deep as I could into the moist grotto. If possible, I would have sunk my entire head into it. Furious sucking on her taut clitoris produced a flow of nectar a thousand times more delectable than that served by Hebe to the gods on Mount Olympus. Some readers may ask what the goddesses drank. They drank from Ganymede's prick, of course.

Madame Dinville was clutching my backside with both her arms while I squeezed her pneumatic buttocks. Her tongue and lips wandered feverishly over my prick while mine did the same to her nether parts. She announced to me the increasing intensity of the raptures I was causing her by convulsive spasms and erratically spreading and closing her thighs. Moderating and augmenting our efforts, we gradually progressed to the peak. We stiffened as if collecting all our faculties to savour the coming bliss to the full.

We discharged simultaneously. From her cunt gushed a torrent of hot delicious fluid which I greedily gulped down. Her mouth was so filled with mine that it took several swallows to get it all down, and she did not release my prick until she was sure that there was not a drop left. The ecstasy vanished, leaving me in despair at the thought it could not be recaptured. But such is carnal pleasure.

Back in the pitiable state from which Madame Dinville's potion had rescued me, I beseeched her to restore me again.

'No, my dear Saturnin,' she replied. 'I love you too much to want to kill you. Be content with the joy we just had.'

Not overly eager to meet my Maker at the expense of another round of pleasure, I followed her example and put on my clothes.

Feeling that Madame Dinville was not displeased with the way I had comported myself, I asked her if I would be permitted to play our games again with her.

'When do you want to come back?' she answered, kissing me on the cheek.

'As soon as I can and that won't be soon enough,' I declared spiritedly. 'How about tomorrow?'

'No,' she smilingly refused me. 'I have to let you get some rest. Come and see me in three days' time.' (She handed me some pastilles that she said would produce the same effect on me as the balm.) 'Be careful how you take them. Also, I don't have to tell you that you are not to say a word about what we did.'

I swore eternal secrecy, and we embraced one last time. So I departed, leaving her under the impression that I had presented her with my virginity.

Fanny Hill's Daughter

Dear Madame:

As you would doubtlessly be the first to inform me, drawing on your own rich experience, there is no certainty in our profession from one hour to the next, let alone for any longer time.

'Twas on the sunniest of afternoons that the dread blow fell. Miss Kitty and I returned from visiting the stores, with our arms full of bundles and anticipating a most lively and pleasant evening, to find my gallant protector's orderly awaiting my arrival in the little room downstairs off the front door. His name was Hogg, and he was sufficient gross to rate it e'en had his parents not wished it on him at birth.

Usually a merry enough dog and inordinately devoted to my master, on this occasion his expression was melancholy enough to wring tears from a statue and aroused in my breast the most exquisite alarm, a sensation soon fully justified by the missive he solemnly handed me.

It was sealed and addressed in my protector's hand, and I feared to open it lest it contain I knew what not awful tidings. Yet mustering my courage under the regard of the devoted Hogg and Miss Kitty, I ripped loose the seal and read—

Most honourable mistress,

It is with the most galling sensations of remorse and regret that I take pen in hand. For ye have brought me nought but pleasure and have merited far more from me than the troubles, self-inflicted by mine own outrageous weaknesse, in which I must now ask you to share . . .

I shall spare you the rest of that awful missive, Madam. Suffice it to say that, in part-payment of a gambling debt contracted at Whyte's my protector had sold me to a Mr Ian MacTavish of Edinburgh.

Nor was I to see my beloved young protector again, for, unable either to face the tragic scenes of parting with my person which must have ensued had he returned to the lodgings we so happily shared till that unhappy day, and being likewise unable to face the thought of forfeiting his honour by refusing to make good the wager he had so rashly entered into and so unhappily lost, he stayed away from my presence, remaining in barracks until I was safely (from his point of vantage) ensconced on the Edinburgh stage two mornings later.

In truth, had it not been for the kind consolations of Miss Kitty, well laced with the sound sensibility that is so much a part of her, I might well have destroyed myself in my grief and terror. For to be thus disposed of, via the turn of a card or the cast of a dye, like a dog or a Blackamoor slave, by a young man to whom I had cheerfully granted my greatest treasures without thought of return . . .

Chere Madame, words fail me!

As it was, had not Miss Kitty reminded me of the cruelty and unfathomable mystery of Man, I must indeed have succumbed. Nor did she content herself with mere verbal solace, but saw to it that my trunks were well filled with furs and furbelows, and that I was further equipped to meet Fortune's whims with two hundred golden guineas and a hamper well stocked with flesh, fowl, chocolate, two bottles of tawny port and other provenances against the rigours of travel—albeit so deep was my distress at the sudden downturn in my fortunes that I was scarce aware of the extent of her assistance.

To Miss Kitty's great kindness, for which I fear I was then insufficiently grateful in my wretched bewilderment, I must, in all good faith and gratitude, add your own sage instruction, Madam, on the frailty of Man and on the readiness of women to expect the worst from these most fickle of all created creatures.

E'en now, I must confess I find it hard to accept the fact that a protector as openly loving and affectionate as Lieutenant the Honourable Roderick Weymiss of His Majesty's Coldstream Guards should venture my person on a play at Whyte's. Is it for such fecklessness and ingratitude that we conceive the creatures in our bellies and give them birth and tender rearing . . .?

But enough of such disgressives, and on with the account of my fortunes.

Of the Honourable Ian MacTavish, my purchaser, I had but little time to record my impressions, for my life with him was of the briefest and least consequential—albeit fraught with the most veritable perils and excitements whilst it endured.

He picked me up in a rented hack two mornings following my receipt of the fateful message from Mr Weymiss, delivered by the porcine Hogg, to convey me to the Edinburgh stage, on which we were to ride in company to the land of Scotland, a land I had never before laid eyes on, and of which I had heard a great many things to make me distrustful, nay even afeard.

The Honourable Mr MacTavish was as tall as a flagpole and as lean as an Irish peasant in a famine year—yet withal not of unprepossessing appearance, save for a great red beak that thrust through and above his muffler like the prow of a Bristol merchantman.

His pale blue eyes looked rheumily down on me, as I stood in Miss Kitty's doorway, surrounded by my trunks, and said to her as she stood beside me, 'Is this the baggage I have engaged?'

In my confusion, I believed he spake not of mine own self but of the trunks, cases and hamper with which mine hostess had so generously provided me. Thus we were off on the wrong foot right away, as I had hardly been accustomed to being thus referred to in front of my face.

But the Honourable Mr MacTavish was no man to stand on argument, and I was whisked away in his rented hack before we had time to exchange so much as a single pleasantry.

All he told me during our half-hour journey to the Royal Scotsman, the tavern whence the Edinburgh stage departed, was, 'If ye'r as plump in bed as Weymiss claims, ye'll hae na troubles with me.'

Which, I must say in all humility, hardly constitutes a wooing, even for a gentleman of Scotland dealing with a young lady of pleasure like myself. Pray tell me if you find it otherwise, Madam, and I shall be more than ever in your debt.

However, if remiss in the courtesies of courtship, my purchaser soon proved himself more than eager in the performance of the role himself, and lived up fully to the reputation of his compatriots from north of the Tyne for ensuring the receipt of that which he had purchased to the final farthing.

For the departure of the coach being delayed due to the tardiness of a passenger of importance, the Honourable Mr MacTavish wasted no time in hustling me into a small room off the ordinary where, by tipping a potboy tuppence, he thought to have privacy in order to, as he bluntly put it, 'try the worth of the goods.'

He made me lie down on a narrow, horsehair couch insufficiently cleansed of the vomit of one or more of the previous eve's revellers, as the noxious fumes that assailed my nostrils made unpleasantly clear, pulled up my petticoats and made ready to enter me without so much as a by-your-leave, unbuttoning his breeches to display a virile member that resembled more the central trunk of a stout bramble bush, so greatly was it knobbed and gnarled, than any organ of Man.

Nor was my already distraught spirit put further at ease when, grasping this ugly but all-too-practical tool in the very nick of time and squeezing its lumpy surface tightly in my fist, it gave evidence of a yellowish discharge that told me all too clearly its owner was suffering from the lesser of those two plagues of Venus that so sorely beleaguer both sexes in the exercise of their natural pleasures, and that in its most active and virulent form.

Having small wish to visit upon mine own self such an unpleasant ailment, I pleaded with him to leave me alone, at least until his trouble had abated, but his blood was up and he was in no mood to brook any delay in seeking immediate satisfaction of his most manly appetite.

Only at the last instant did I recollect the trick of

which you must be well aware, and in which Madame Berkeley schooled me, the trick of knocking the large vein in the side of the prick with a fingernail, thus causing the sturdiest of male emblems to resume its sorriest condition (not that the condition of my new protector's was not sorry enough to begin with).

In any event, he subsided, albeit with wrath, and made for to strike me with his stick, uttering great outcries about insubordination and ingratitude to which I paid small heed. I stood up to him, however, and informed him in no uncertain terms that I would announce to the world his condition and what he intended doing to me whilst in it—at which he resigned himself to muttering fury and, at last, rebuttoned his breeches to my great relief.

Had I but a moment further in which to ponder my plight, I doubt not that I should have left him then and there, and let my recent protector get out of his debt of honour to the MacTavish as best he could.

But all my possessions, save the golden sovereigns in my purse (which was concealed in my muff) and the clothes I wore on my back, were already aboard the Edinburgh stage, and I had small desire to render myself once more destitute in so short an interval of time. On top of this, the Eminent Gentleman for whom the stage was held arrived, and demanded we be off at once, as he was in a great hurry to tend to his affairs in the north. So I was bundled aboard with little chance to speak, or even determine, mine own mind.

Ne'er in all my born days did ever I see a gentleman of such surpassing ugliness as this Eminent Gentleman, who took a seat directly opposite me, resting his chin on his elegant knuckles and his elegant

knuckles on the carved ivory top of his elegant ebony
cane, splaying wide his knees with utter disregard of
the comfort of those passengers who sat on either side
of him.

Save for the ruffles at his wrists and throat, he
was attired wholly in black broadcloth, his gentility
attested to by his total lack of jewelled adornment (for
certes none but a very great gentleman has courage
thus to appear in public without evidence of his property in jewellery or insignia of some sort). Only his
buckles were of fine, polished silver that winked reflec-
tion of each passing sunbeam that entered the stage-
coach windows as we jogged along, drearily enough,
over the rough surface of the St. Alban's road.

His face, beneath his great black cocked hat, which
filled with gloom that entire portion of the stage in
which he sat, like some gigantic bird of melancholy
prey, was lined and seemed, as if carved in putty by
some overzealous Canova, and his deep-sunk eyes
remained fixed on my face and person as if held there
by a lodestone. So ugly, in truth, was this august
personage, that my new protector, the Honourable
Mr MacTavish, appeared actually young and handsome in comparison.

Mr MacTavish was all too evidently impressed by
the honour of riding with so obvious a Personage of
Importance. Albeit I was considerably taken up by
the evident interest which the eminent stranger took
in my person (which he made no effort at all to hide),
I could not but be aware of the starts and fidgets of
my new protector as that worthy conjured up conver-
sational opening gambits, only to decide that each in
turn was not a proper ploy and remain silent, his

mouth opening and closing like that of a goldfish swimming idly in its bowl.

Not until we were more than an hour beyond Charing Cross did Mr MacTavish find his gambit and seize upon it. Our coach had just travelled over a pot-hole which caused it to tip so severely that we were all but hurled into one another's laps, all save the elegant stranger, whose cane, firmly planted on the floor of the stage, held him firm as Gibraltar itself against the human tide that assailed his flanks.

In overt admiration, my protector then addressed himself directly to *l'eminence noir*, remarking, 'I'll wager ye'r no descendant of King Canute, sirrah, for, mighty monarch that he was, with all his powers he was unable to halt th'advance of the waters.'

Save for a single eyebrow, which rose mayhap a half-finger, the elegant stranger in black gave no response—at which, believing him deaf, my protector repeated his words, shouting at the top of his lungs.

The stranger flinched ever so slightly. He removed one smoothly gloved hand to the ear nearest the MacTavish and patted it lightly, as if to be certain the appendage remained yet in place and attached to his head.

Then, employing an utterly world-weary drawl and pronouncing his syllables as if he were addressing a child, the eminent one spake to me and remarked, 'If ye'r companion is addressing himself to me, I'll thank ye to translate his words—for surely, with all those rolls of his rrr's, he employs some barbarous *patois* which I, alas, find myself utterly unable to comprehend.'

I had noted my new protector's heavy Scottish burr, but had lacked either the wit or courage to call him on it as this stranger did. At which The MacTavish grew so incensed that he roared it a third time, in the voice of a Caledonian lion, if indeed such a creature exists.

The elegant eyebrow went up again, the wearied lips pursed slightly, and the gentleman in black uttered a single syllable directed at me . . . '*Please!*'

So I repeated it more gently for him, at which he afforded me a tiny smile of such confidential import (as if, indeed, we shared a secret from which the rest of the world was locked out) that his ugliness quite vanished beneath the assurance and glow of his personality.

Then at last he replied, in the most exquisitely insolent drawl imaginable, ' 'Tis well for you that no wager exists, for ye'd have lost, my dear fellow. I'm a descendant of the late King Canute on the side of my great-great grandmother, thirty-three times removed, and have in my house a small bucket of that very sand which was wet by the tide that refused to obey his royal command. Should ye care to call and view it, ye'll find it still damp.'

'Had I wagered, I'd hae won, sirrah,' cried my protector, now beside himself with fury. 'Damp or not, ye'll have difficulty proving the sand was not culled from the sands of the Thames only last week.'

'If ye please, my dear, will you again translate?' the gentleman in black inquired of me, and of course I complied, enjoying my rude protector's exposure for the man of ill parts he most assuredly was (may his soul rest in Presbyterian peace, where'er it lies!).

When I had finished, he smiled at me again in confidence, and replied, 'Tell the good fellow then, sweet lady, that he'll have just as de'il a time proving th'opposite. *Hah*!'

With this, the elegant gentleman in black, disregarding the MacTavish's apoplectic sounds of stuttering fury no more than t'were the lullaby of a nursing mother, composed his chin upon his knuckles once again and, after one slow wink at me, closed both his eyes and, to all appearances, fell fast asleep, in which condition he remained despite the rude jolting of the stage until our halt for dinner at St. Alban's, whereat he disappeared into a private room, while my discomfited protector could not bring himself to spend more upon our fare than was afforded by the ordinary.

At this, once again, I was reminded of the parsimony for which the Scottish folk are all too well renowned, and began to fret myself anew about th'uncertainties of my present estate. Furthermore, I wondered how a man to whom even a farthing appeared so dear had discovered the courage necessary to play for high stakes at Whyte's.

As yet, the problem appeared unanswerable, and I could but lament inwardly over the cruel twist of fortune that had served to place me, helpless, in his niggardly claws.

My hopes that he might prove a protector of weak or lagging appetite vanished as I watched him dismember the joint placed before us, and gobble it so rudely that I was forced to feed upon scraps left swimming in the grease and gravy.

Nor did he forego the pleasures of the bottle (since all drink, like all food consumed along the way was included in our passage). Yet this latter proved, in truth a blessing, for so deeply did he indulge that he soon fell asleep and snored loudly upon my shoulder virtually all the way to Luton, at which town, bone-weary, we alighted for supper and to pass the night.

It was here that a most curious happening occurred, one which has since proved all-important in its influence upon my present fortunes and estate.

My protector and I retired to a private room (it appeared that, for once, the greater parsimony of displaying me, his most expensive purchase, in the ordinary after dark or sleeping with other passengers and paying guests in one of the common bedrooms, overcame the lesser parsimony of paying extra for more secluded lodgings), where I steeled myself to endure the inevitable and, again in accord with my wise training for a young woman like myself to put the best face possible upon it.

Yet my apprehensions were to prove groundless, for even while we dozed and jolted in the stage en route to my northern exile, a kindly Providence, assisted by a more earthly agency, was moving in my behalf. At first alighting and retiring to our chamber, we were both so boneweary and travel-fatigued that our only thoughts were of easing our aching flesh and bones and of removing the dust and stains of our journey (at least myself, for the MacTavish shewed neither desire nor inclination toward cleanliness).

A scullery girl fetched me two pails of steaming hot water (for which my protector, grumbling at such extravagance, forced me to pay myself out of mine own small store of silver), in which, with the aid of a cloth and soap, I was able to wash after a fashion. Ye may be sure I took care not to remove any essential articles of clothing lest, despite his groans of aching weariness, I should arouse his lust prematurely.

The tavern food proving unsuited to his palate

(and, it must be confessed, to mine own as well), the MacTavish fell to demolishing the contents of the hamper with which Miss Kitty had provided me to such hearty avail that soon all that remained were a few oddments of bone and gristle, and mayhap, a few fingers in one of the two bottles of tawny port.

At this point, my protector felt quite well disposed toward me (and why not?), offering me praises for having come so well provided with sustenance, and belching his appreciation. He laid hands upon me as if to buss me in fatherly fashion (yet the manner in which his hands strayed to the roundness of my breasts and buttocks and lingered there gave me cause to doubt that his affections were wholly paternal in aim or origin), vowing that ne'er had mortal man been blessed with such a bonny mistress.

At this point, there came a knocking at the door of the room, and with a curse at such untimeliness, my protector reluctantly moved to answer it.

A manservant stood there, bearing a tray on which stood a cobwebbed bottle of fine old scotch whiskey, and a note. The manservant stood there, awaiting an answer, while The MacTavish scanned it and remarked, ' 'Tis indeed an unco display of courtesy on the part of your master. Pray gie him my thanks and appreciation.'

Impassively, the manservant replied, 'Mr Selwyn requested me to inform you, sir, that upon my return to his quarters, he will toast your health from the contents of a like bottle and wishes you to do the same for him.'

'Tell him his wish is fulfilled,' said my protector. 'You might add that I feel in no way discountenanced, upon learning his identity, at having been bested in verbal intercourse today by a gentleman of such renowned wit.'

When the manservant had gone, The MacTavish, all aglow at having received such a tribute (to say nothing of free whiskey), pulled out the cork and poured a stout measure into one of the wineglasses, lifted it to its donor and downed it straightaway.

'*Wurragh!* 'Tis powerful stuff!' he gasped, shuddering throughout his entire great frame as it went down. His eyes turned on me, bright red from the effusion of blood brought on by the force of his reaction, and he opened his ugly mouth to speak whereat to me.

Yet, once again, he was speechless, as on the coach that morning. For his face went slack, his eyes rolled upward, and he fell prone upon the carpet with a horrid sound and a shaking of the building itself.

I was hard-put to it to know what to do, but before I could cry out for help, the manservant had reopened the door and, putting a finger to his lips, enjoined me to silence. Nodding in satisfaction at sight of my unconscious protector, he removed the bottle of whiskey and the glass from which the MacTavish had drank and, placing them under one arm, offered me the other.

'My master awaits ye, ma'am,' he said with great courtesy. 'Permit me to shew ye to him.'

I hesitated, fearing dire consequences from the unexpected action I had so recently witnessed, and said, 'What have ye done to him?' Is he dead?'

'Only till morning, ma'am,' replied the manservant. 'And when he awakens, I'll warrant his head and stomach contain far too many woes for him to think of anything else for another twenty-four hours.'

Still I hesitated, but not for long. After all, my present situation was hardly one to my liking, and almost any change in protectors was bound to be for the better. So I said, 'My things! I cannot leave them behind. Nor can I well hope to return to my gentleman after this. He'd think me guilty of complicity and have my hide.'

'Ye'r things I'll see to myself at once,' he promised. Then, eyeing me, 'As to ye'r beautiful hide, I'm certain my master will treat it with proper affection and tenderness.'

'You are insolent,' I told him, smiling, for his good humour was infectious.

'Ain't it in truth a terrible thing?' he countered with feigned remorse. Nor was I surprised to learn that his name was Patrick.

The chamber to which Patrick took me was—need I say it?—far more roomy and sumptuously furnished than that which the penny-pinching MacTavish had hired for the night. It was well carpeted and held a large four-poster bed and a number of tables and chairs, as well as an elegant commode disguised as a low-boy. In the most comfortable of the armchairs sat my *vis-a-vis* of the stage still fully attired in his elegant black travelling clothes, at his elbow on a large tray the remains of a comfortable repast.

Eyeing me with the closest attention, he smiled and said, 'I trust a change of companions does not meet with ye'r disapproval, my dear. I must say that ye'r a most uncommon fine young woman, mightily ill-matched indeed with that barbarous Scotsman ye wore on ye'r elbow.'

Albeit I am well and dutifully aware of the fact that girlish ways sit ill with the deportment of a mature young lady, as I by now bethought myself, there was that in my new friend's manner and delivery that forbade me aught but to giggle most unbecomingly. The mere thought that I had been wearing The MacTavish on my elbow proved beyond resisting.

Mercifully, Mr Selwyn, for such was his name, did not appear displeased by my reaction, albeit he failed to respond in kind. A sparkle in his eye informed me that he enjoyed my pleasure.

When I could speak, I said most demurely, 'Milord, it would ill become me to show disrespect for the gentleman who gained my person fair and square.'

'My I inquire just how this ill-favoured son of Caledonia won ye?' He inquired. 'And do not call me milord, for I am not of the peerage.'

'Pray then, how shall I address you?' I inquired.

The faint smile reappeared. 'Ye may call me Mr Selwyn,' he replied most graciously. 'And may I reiterate my question?'

'I was informed by messenger, but two days ago, that my master lost me to The MacTavish at picquet—at Whyte's.'

He studied me in silence before remarking, 'By Gad, ye must be Roddy Weymiss' woman! He spake mightily well of ye before he pressed his luck too far.'

I lowered mine eyes with what I hoped was becoming modesty, and Mr Selwyn paused to inhale a pinch of snuff, which he withdrew from a most elegant chased-silver box adorned with rubies and sapphires. He uttered a snorting sound, which I at first mistook to be a sneeze, but which I realized later was his manner of laughter—for Mr Selwyn *never* sneezes whilst taking snuff, a reaction he holds to be most vulgar.

In kindly tone, he said, 'The young idiot! Risking such a prize on the turn of a card!' Then, after a pause, 'Well Weymiss' loss, Selwyn's gain.' And, in a most considerate manner, 'My dear, please tell me frankly and with the utmost candour—has any warm sentiment developed between the man MacTavish and ye'rself in the course of ye'r brief acquaintanceship?'

I replied. 'Tis most thoughtful of you to ask, Mr Selwyn, for indeed such a sentiment has indeed developed, at least as regards my feelings for Mr MacTavish.'

'*Amazing*!' An expression of regret flickered over his impassive features, to be followed by one of incredulity. 'I find it hard to believe, my dear—nor do I mean to cast any doubt upon ye'r truthfulness. But with such a man in so short a time. . . .'

'None the less, 'tis true,' I replied. 'I developed the warmest hatred for Mr MacTavish that I have ever conceived for any human being.'

'That, my dear,' he said, permitting himself a smile of pure relief, 'deserves a toast. Will ye join me?'

'I'd like nothing better,' I replied, and at Mr Selwyn's bidding, Patrick fetched glasses and poured us both full measures of whiskey from a bottle that looked suspiciously similar to that which the MacTavish had drunk the gift-draught that laid him low.

'Fear not,' said Mr Selwyn, reading my mind all too accurately. 'Better yet, let Patrick drink from ye'r glass, since he is playing a part in our little comedy.'

'Indeed he has—a part for which I am most grateful,' I told them.

'Ah, Patrick's important scene is yet to be

41

performed,' said Mr Selwyn. We looked on while the burly manservant drained my tumbler and received its contents with no visible ill-effect—after which, Mr. Selwyn and I drank a toast proposed by Mr Selwyn, to a hope that the MacTavish slumber long and soundly through the remainder of the night.

We drank another toast to my comeliness soon after, in which I was happy to join, then a toast to the recent good fortune of Mr Selwyn (by which, I took it to mean his good fortune was the acquisition of mine own poor self), the while Patrick was absent from the chamber upon some business his master proposed.

Upon his return, my new protector, (for such I rightly took him to be) said to his man, 'Patrick, are ye ready to play the game?'

' 'Twill be a pleasure sir,' replied Patrick, his dark eyes devouring me with what I felt to be unseemly lust in the presence of his master.

Then, turning to me, Mr Selwyn said, 'I trust ye'll not be offended, but I have found it to my advantage to adopt a most wise and intelligent policy of the Empress Catherine of Russia.'

'Indeed, Mr Selwyn . . . ?' I spake warily, for I could feel it in the atmosphere of the room that some most unusual request was about to be made of me.

'She maintains at her court in St. Petersburg a most accomplished young Scottish peeress who bears the nickname of *l'epreuveuse*—the tester. Whenever the Empress desires a member of her bodyguard or of a visiting embassy, she first sends this woman to his bed to discover if he has the qualities requisite to the Empress' own pleasure. 'Tis said both women are of a remarkable similarity in this regard, just as Patrick and I are as like as peas in a pod.'

'You wish me to bed with Patrick before bedding me yourself?' I asked.

'If ye do not wish to be returned to the tender mercies of Mr MacTavish,' Mr Selwyn replied, most gently withal, yet with unmistakable intent. 'In any event, I'd see you naked before going on with the game, my dear, if only to ensure the genuineness of ye'r indubitable charms.'

In truth, I was in no way displeased at the prospect of displaying my charms and accomplishments for the edification of so amiable and elegant a gentleman as Mr Selwyn, but I could not resist casting a sidelong glance at the manservant who was to put me to the test and said, 'If Patrick is willing. . . .'

My new protector, Mr Selwyn, is not a man who gives way to laughter upon slight pretext. He has since told me on many an occasion that it well behooves a gentleman who would be considered so by his peers to display any emotion at all, either in public or private. Yet, at my poor foolish remark, he put back his well-powdered hair, opened his mouth and gave vent to a series of bellows and roars that momentarily alarmed me lest he had suffered some sort of fit, until I saw the tears streaming down his cheeks.

Nor, *chère madame*, could I perceive why my innocent jest should have given rise to such an extreme reaction, albeit within minutes I got the full point in more senses than one. For, having removed my clothes and posed prettily before Mr Selwyn, who ogled my dugs, my belly and my cunny as if he had ne'er before viewed their like (which, indeed, he has since claimed he never did), I turned toward Patrick, who came up

43

beside me and discovered that the Hibernian was not only willing but ready.

Madam, ne'er in all my born days did I see such a tool. Where Lieutenant the Honourable Roderick Weymiss' shaft was long and rifle-thin, and that of his boon companion, Lord Peter Ronsabell's was short and thick as a Coehorn, Patrick's was their combined match in both dimensions. One glance at its immensity, and I shuddered at the thought of so massive an instrument probing my delicate inner parts, and would have protested its entry vigorously had opportunity but offered.

For the rest, Patrick was stoutly made, and his bones well coated with smooth flesh bearing but little hair—all told a most attractive couch companion albeit I found it difficult to contemplate any portion of him at that moment save the alarming codpiece I was destined to contain. I felt the great strength of him as he plucked me from the carpet like a piece of cloth and laid me on my backside on the unopened bed—whose tufted spread did threaten under the pressure of our combined weights to dot my tender flesh with more dimples than nature e'er intended.

Patrick toyed with my tits and cunny skilfully enough to prepare us both for combat, and I encircled his mighty lance with a timorous fist, nor were my fears in any way allayed by the fact that palm and fingers could scarce encompass its girth. Albeit I did my best to guide the purple crocus blossom of his stout maypole within the portals of my cunny, terror forbade mine own juices greasing the mouth of the tunnel, and his best efforts availed him nothing.

Undeterred, he laughed and kissed and cozened me as I were a doll, so helpless did he hold me in the strength of his embrace, ultimately upending me and rolling beneath till I full straddled him with his mighty blossom still prodding amain at my un-oiled gates. Whereat he unleashed his hold of my waist with one hand and put it to his mouth and spat upon it gently. He then slid it beneath my centre-piece and annointed his great mace, then held me as in a gentle vice and lowered me slowly upon it . . . and, *lo*! almost ere I knew what was happening, his crocus was well within my tunnel and forcing its way slowly upward into the very heart of me.

I cried out as its great girth bid fair to stretch my poor passageway past the bursting point, and looked at Mr Selwyn for aid, but that gentleman's eyes were glued upon the *pièce de resistance* of our performance, and he neither saw nor heard my plea for mercy. His eyes were fixed on our fused centre parts as if they were about to pop like great ripe currents from their caverns in his skull.

So great, indeed, was my discomfort, that I wriggled with all my might to escape the agony of my impalement upon Patrick's giant codpiece, and thereby was either done or undone depending upon the eye of the beholder—for the motion involved caused my juices to start flowing in a great suffusion, and what had been a mortal agony was transformed quicker than words can say it into a delight beyond any I had known before and scarce to be endured.

I cried out again, but not for succour this time as nature and Sir Isaac Newton's Law of Gravity caused Patrick's penetration of my poor small body to become deeper still, and our most private hairs met and mingled in the broth and froth of our passion. I soon felt his rigidity increase, and his machine grow turgid until it bucked within me, and his love-juice spurted to rebound from the very top of my womb, whereat he, too, cried out and fell limp, and what had so short a time before filled me with discomfort beyond endurance soon dwindled till it threatened to leave behind an empty, gaping void no more to be borne than its impalement.

With gentle moans, I settled myself more closely still upon his waning member, rubbing and rotating mine own private parts around it until, as if by magic, its retreat was stemmed, and soon a rally got under way again filling me to a bursting point I no longer feared or wished to avoid—quite the opposite, I confess it.

Resting a moment after the rebirth was complete, I looked again at Mr Selwyn and laughed and thrust out my tongue at him, a gesture my elegant new protector, with the most seemly gravity, returned in kind, thereby causing me to love him the more dearly. But at this point, Patrick returned to life with a great upward movement in a circular motion that sent reason, in truth all other sense and sensibility, dancing merrily away, and we clouted and clipped and clasped and clambered upon one another like mad moujhicks from Tartary's plain indulging in some heathen ritual wherein cunny and codpiece replace the altar of our Lord.

Since Patrick had already discharged his cannon once full within me, his powder took far longer to ignite on the second round of pleasure, and we worked one another over vigorously with the utmost delight until it seemed we would fair be drowned in our own sweat and other effusions, and sheer mutual exhaustion bid fair to put an end to our pleasure without its appointed conclusion, at least as far as stout Patrick was concerned, for I must confess, *chère madame*, that I attained paradise so many times I felt myself threatened with becoming a permanent resident of that celestial sphere.

Then, with a mighty heaving and thrusting and groaning, my tester achieved that which he so vigorously sought, and this time I was far too spent to seek to retain his spear at rigid attention within me, nor could I have done so e'en had I possessed the strength.

When we had rested for a while, drained of all desire, and naked on the spread that now resembled an ocean in mighty turmoil, so great was its confusion, rather than the calm sea it had been at the outset of our great trial, Mr Selwyn most considerately asked Patrick if he felt me qualified to service the master as well as the man. To which, Patrick could reply but with a heart-felt groan, at which Mr Selwyn professed himself entirely satisfied, as he was with what he had witnessed of our protracted bout.

He then had me bathe and e'en towelled me off afterward himself, paying especial attention to those parts of my poor body that had been most actively engaged, and pronouncing them charming. Whereat he told me I must dress, for that we had a hard journey still ahead of us that night.

'I am not afeard of your MacTavish,' he assured me solemnly. ' 'Tis just that I have long since learned to deem discretion in these matters by far the better part of valour.'

'As ye wish,' I replied, not even wondering what new turn my fortune was to take, so spent, was I from my two turns with Patrick, and, rendered so languid by the warm water of the bath Mr Selwyn had had the tavern scullery maid heat and pour.

Had he suggested we take off for Timbucktoo itself, I doubt not that I should have assented without question. So I dressed with such care as conditions permitted and accompanied him downstairs in the inn.

Patrick awaited us, on the box of a three-quarter-front carriage, and I must confess myself both relieved and mightily impressed to discover my dunnage securely strapped, along with Mr Selwyn's, on the rack at the rear. My heart went out both to my new protector and to his man for affording me a symptom of their care and comfort in regard to myself, as well as for the pleasures the man had afforded me in the inn. Forsooth, any fretting that might have troubled me at forming an alliance with a man as obviously mature as Mr Selwyn was allayed by recollection of how inexhaustibly his servant could minister to my needs and foibles, so much so that any lingering sorrow at loss of Lieutenant the Honourable Roderick Weymiss and his charming companions was quite allayed.

Maudie

After dinner that night Charlie begged to be excused. Sitting alone in the little smoking-room, he began to think out his plans.

At that moment one of the pretty maids came in without knocking.

'Oh, mistress's compliments, sir, and she'd forgotten to give you the key of the wine and spirit cupboards; there they are. I'll open them.'

She brought out the necessaries, also a pile of books.

'Mistress says you might like these, too,' she giggled. 'Let me show you the best,' and she flicked over the pages of an obviously very erotic book, full of coloured plates of lust in every form. 'Saucy, aren't they? Look at this.'

It portrayed three couples, hopelessly mixed up, tongues, lips, cocks and cunts in helpless and joyful confusion.

She put her hand on Charlie's shoulder, playfully flicking his ear, and bending over kissed his forehead, pressing her breasts against the back of his head.

'I'm glad you've come,' she cooed; 'so are all the girls. We like you. I'm going to bring your hot water up to-night; mind you're awake.'

Charlie couldn't help it. He pulled her round on to his knee. She put his hand under her clothes herself, and wriggled.

'It's all right,' she said; 'no one will come in. This is what I'm best at,' and she slipped between his legs and undid the fly buttons with her teeth.

'You little devil!' was all Charlie could say.

A confused, gurgling noise was the only answer—his prick seemed to be half way down her throat.

He nervously fingered her head—she had deliciously soft hair—and gave himself to an abandon of lust.

She gently tickled his balls till his cock seemed to throb like a motor bicycle engine, and, well, it couldn't last for ever; he spent like Niagara.

The pretty girl threw back her head and gulped it down.

'I say, old chap,' came Tubby's voice from behind, 'you're beginning soon, y'know, and you've got the nicest, by God, y'have, and, I say, your aunt's looking for you, and she's going to stay the night, and what the devil are we going to do, what, what!'

The pretty maid stood up, blushing, and hung her head.

'You'd better be off, my dear,' said Tubby; 'and, for heavens sake, be careful what you do or say when that old lady's in the house.'

When they were alone, Charlie apologised.

'Oh, don't worry about *that*, old chap. You can do what you like to the girls, but it's your aunt—quick, for God's sake put those books away: I hear a rustle.'

Charlie was just in time. Lady Lavinia was in the room just as the cupboard door slammed.

She sniffed at the collection of liquors.

'As I thought, drinking, and *solitary* drinking. Why couldn't you be like your friend and come in the drawing-room for a little music?

'And what's this?' She picked up a maid's cap from

51

the floor. 'One of the *servant's* caps! What's it doing here?'

'Oh, I suppose she must have dropped it,' answered Charlie, pettishly. 'I'll come down to the drawing-room now. It'll be bed-time in a few minutes.'

In the servants' quarters of the house, discussion as to the identity and *raison d'être* of the new guests ran rife.

Young men of the world like Charlie were no new thing, but Aunt Lavinia—in such a house—well!

'Such particular instructions I've had to clear her room of anything saucy,' said the old housekeeper, gossiping in her room with the butler and the chauffeur; 'and I'm to take 'er tea myself: let none of them 'ussies go near.

'It makes me fair nervous, it do. Not that I altogether 'old with these games 'ere, but we're all in it, with our eyes open—oh, dear, *if* she should see some of them pictures.'

''Twould be a to-do, and no error,' said the butler.

'And the good lady she tink Mr Bertie so good young man vos—ha! ha!' and the chauffeur laughed viciously. 'She into what you call a 'ornet's nest got, is it not?'

In the greater servants' hall speculation was also rife: guests seldom arrived at that house except in very large parties, in motor loads at a time, as a rule. And as for mistress bringing home a single young man, she hadn't done such a thing for years.

No one had seen his condition when he arrived except the chauffeur, who had maintained a dogged silence. He had been told to do so, and his job was too good to lose.

They were a free and easy lot in the upper servants' hall at Maudie's, with a very large preponderance of women, mere girls, many of them, and all pretty. In fact, the house was ridiculously over-stocked with females. There was nothing for them to do save when the very big parties were on, and then they were more required for the photography than anything else.

There were only two men, both deft-handed servants, and both French, and a French-American cook, who was rather a wet blanket on the general irresponsibility of the girls. There remained the page-boy, and several other young boys and girls who helped in the scullery.

The girls did not care much for the two Frenchmen, and the cook thought of nothing at all but inventing new dishes; hence the joy with which Charlie was received.

It was an appetising scene. Everything in the house was done, and the girls sprawled in varied alluring *déshabillés*—it was a hot night, and drawers and chemise, or chemise only, or drawers and vest, and one or two, vest only. Two were quite naked. The room was very comfortable to lounge in, and Maudie didn't care what happened so long as she was waited on quickly. Two girls remained dressed, ready to see their mistress and Lady Lavinia to bed when rung for.

The page-boy was in general request, fetching coffee and cigarettes, and came in for a good deal more petting than was good for him. In fact, he was quite *blasé*. The warm caress of a semi-naked divinity had *no* effect on him.

They disappeared to bed by degrees, till only Elsie and May were left.

'Are you going to take the new gentleman any hot water?' queried May.

'Yes,' answered Elsie.

It was she who had come into the smoking-room.

'May I follow you?'

'A good half-hour after me. I tell you, dear, I need something badly; I haven't had my legs opened for a week, and it's just about time. You come in later, and we'll see what the two of us can't make him do: he's got a rare big 'un.'

'Right'—and they sealed the compact with a kiss.

There are few things prettier than the sight of two pretty women who are both lustful, and who really care for each other, kissing as if they meant it.

Tubby rolled over in bed, and grunted, then he kissed his bedfellow, and was immediately asleep. Maudie sighed. She had had a great deal too much of this of late. She thought over the events of the day, and longed for Charlie. For one wild moment she recollected how firmly Tubby slept, and contemplated making a dash for Charlie's room—but prudence prevailed. She mustn't jeopardize the future. She took up a book, *Nadia*, a lustful romance, and tried to read herself to sleep, but in vain. Her blood boiled, and at last she woke up Tubby roughly.

'Tubby, dear, I *must* and *will* be fucked,' she said. 'You hardly ever touch me, and yet you expect me to be true to you. Come on.'

Tubby acquiesced sadly. His extreme stoutness made it quite impossible for him to attack in the old Adam and Eve fashion. He had to do it as the beast of the field. He got out of bed and turned Maudie over its edge. Then, without seeming in the slightest enraptured by the sight of her snowy white buttocks, he deliberately plunged his sausage-like machine into that gap which should only have been reserved for connoisseurs.

Of course he liked it: he was very healthy, and full of good food and wine, and his penis swelled enormously as his strokes increased in vigour. Maudie lay on her stomach, her pretty little face buried in the lace-edged pillow, and her brain, behind her closed eyes, just a blissful vision of Charlie.

Oh! if it had only been Charlie!

The fact is known that sometimes women who, when madly lustful for particular men, are forced to be carnal elsewhere, derive really more pleasure from the beautific dream of their fancied darling, who in a vision is responsible for the flesh spasms which the unseen operator manipulates, than they do when the real darling is in the saddle, so to speak.

Maudie certainly loved it, and she was only just conscious enough of what had happened to bite her tongue to stop crying 'Charlie' as the last violent stroke from her fat lover sent a hard-shot torrent right up to the doors of her womb.

'My God,' she thought, 'I really believe Tubby has copped me this time.'

She hastened to syringe, a precaution she seldom took with her fat lover.

Tubby, on his part, sank exhausted into an armchair.

'You've fair whacked me this time, petlet,' he gasped. 'I've never had a fuck like this with you before. What's come over you?'

The dream was still in Maudie's brain as she answered vaguely, 'How—how can you help it, when you love so much?'

When Tubby did turn off to sleep he dreamed rapturously. Maudie, too, slept well: she was thoroughly tired at last. These physical and mental fucks combined are pretty fairly damaging to the vitality.

Lady Lavinia, when the pretty maid had helped her out of her clothes and given her a nightdress, the decorations of which ill coincided with the elderly widow, removed her wig, put her teeth in a glass, and sniffed round the room.

She could not but approve of the comfort. No detail necessary to coax comfort to the weary or lazy bed-goer was missing.

Maudie had put it to her very delicately that if she had neuralgia—or anything—there was 'something' in the cupboard.

She had a look, and found, in addition to the 'something', a pile of books, one of which she picked out at random.

It was prettily bound, and called *Nemesis Hunt*. She took it back to bed with her, had a very hearty drop of the 'something', and opened it.

A good many readers of this book may have read *Nemesis Hunt*. They will remember that that charming and loquacious lady somewhat lets the tail go with the hide in her confessions. A fuck is called a fuck, and there is *more* than fucking in the naïve three volumes.

Lady Lavinia's eyes dilated as she read. Once before, in the very early days of her married life, she had been shown a book like this by her husband, and she remembered now, with a sigh, *what* a night they had subsequently had.

Her first impulse was to throw down the book in anger, the consciousness of her position, her reputation, flashed through her brain, but—curiosity prevailed, and Lady Lavinia, firmly adjusting her glasses, took another strong sip of the 'something', and started seriously in to read the first volume of *The Confessions of Nemesis Hunt*.

When young, she had been very pretty, and had been much courted. She had loved admiration, and had flirted above a bit.

Her short married life with the late earl had been a long round of love and lust, and frank sexual enjoyment, but his sudden death had brought about an equally sudden revulsion of feeling.

Lady Lavinia had turned suddenly very good, mid-Victorian good. She had mourned her husband, and put a great deal of mournfulness into other people's lives by doing so—as have other illustrious widows.

Now there came back a rush of something—it must have been Georgian—and she let down the drawbridge.

At the end of the fifteenth page of Nemesis Hunt's pleasant confessions, she decided to leave on the morrow, *but* return.

Nemesis was put under the pillow, and in that very ultra-modern house there slept what may be described as a memory of Cremorne.

Charlie Osmond went to bed with mixed feelings. He had had a very good time: he had a prospect of future life in view, which he rather welcomed—*but*, he wanted to be with Maudie—not to be immoral, but to talk. It flatly bored him to go to bed.

Outside, the Thames valley looked very peaceful. The dogs, the chickens, everything slept, except Charlie, *and* Elsie and May, who, after seeing to the little wants of Lady Lavinia and Maudie, bided their time for an invasion into Charlie's room.

That worthy had his suspicions of impending events. He did not lock the door, but sat by the window in his pyjamas, and gazed peacefully out over the moonlit garden and river.

It was altogether rather too nice, too idyllic, and—well—the door opened, and Elsie came in without knocking.

She was fully dressed, and carried a tray with hot water and glasses.

Charlie laughed.

'I somehow expected you,' he said; 'but do you know it's very wrong. You don't know what I am, whether I'm married or not, or *what* trouble this might get me into.'

Elsie laughed.

'Well, I've done it,' she said. 'I meant to from the first moment I saw you. Give me a cigarette and a drink, and let me come and sit in the window, and you won't be bored for the next half hour, I can promise you.'

Elsie curled up on the corner of the window-seat, the moon full on her delicate little features, lit the proffered Albany cigarette, sipped a little of the whisky and Rosbach, and grinned, frankly grinned.

'I suppose you think it frightful cheek,' she suggested.

'Well, I can't say I don't like your cheek,' and he kissed it.

Elsie kissed him back on the lips, and took off her bodice. She had very pretty arms, and a gold bangle with a purple enamel medallion, worn just above the left elbow, did not make them less attractive.

She had a little more of the Three Star Bushmills, stood up and slid her skirt off: then her chemise—she wore no petticoats—and to cut a long story short, her next sitting-place was on Charlie's knee, and the next kiss had nothing to do with cheeks.

Charlie lifted her on to the bed. Even then, though she was exasperatingly pretty, he could not help thinking of Maudie.

She curled over him, slowly, deliberately and maliciously taking both his hands in hers, and rubbing her soft cheeks against his.

There must be something in telepathy, for at the moment, the precise moment that Charlie reconciled himself to a connection which he *knew* would be nice, but which he really did not want, save for the exquisite pleasure in thinking that Elsie's arms were Maudie's, that latter lady saw in a blue mist of ecstacy the image of a very loving Charlie—poor Tubby being merely the engine-driver who drove the imagination of her recklessly lustful brain.

Charlie let himself frankly go. There was no light in the room at all bar the shafts of the moon, filtering through the swaying trees. The silhouetted skyline and the delightfully placid atmosphere made Charlie lazy.

He had some recollection of little tickling fingers swiftly undoing the strings of his pyjamas, little tickling fingers also playing with an already erect member, naked arms twisted round his neck, firm, plump legs twisted round his thighs, and—well—he was in—well in—and those soft cheeks were most lustfully pressed to his.

Maudie had been very loving, *but*—all said and done—as he felt all his love juice being sucked out of him, *this*, Charlie couldn't help admitting, was better still.

He came in a long rhapsody: the girl jerked the eiderdown over them, and snuggled up. He didn't know whether she meant to stay the night, or not, or what the morals of this peculiar house permitted, but it was *very* comfortable.

He was just going to sleep when the door opened very quietly, and *another* girl came into the moonlight.

Charlie gave up. He remembered where he was, and determined to die game. The 'other girl' apologised laughingly, and the original giggled in the sheets.

'You don't mind May, do you?' she said.

'No,' was Charlie's answer; 'but it's got to stop at May, you and May. If I've got to go through the whole *personnel* of the establishment, I give up.'

May did not answer—but just, just seemed to *slide* just as Elsie had done—out of her clothes, and into bed.

Poor, but happy Charlie—he realized quite what a squeezed lemon must feel like—but he valiantly did his duty.

May was more placid than Elsie, more tender, more caressing, perhaps, but Charlie's cock was just as stiff as he felt his balls right against the soft buttocks of his new love.

It was a long fuck and a delightful one. Elsie, wicked little devil, gave every help in her power.

She flung back the clothes, and there they lay, three naked bodies in the moonlight. There was no artificial light save the glow of Elsie's cigarette end.

Elsie slipped the pillow down so that her little friend's bottom was just correctly raised, and, as Charlie knelt between May's legs, guided his penis dexterously in.

May, of course, was shaved, in the fashion of everyone in Maudie's mansion, and Charlie began more and more to appreciate the added charm of the hairless cunt, as he thrust his fingers between their bodies and felt the soft, warm, smooth flesh.

Elsie crept right on top of them, her head between Charlie's legs, so that her tongue swept over and over his swelling balls. As his cock slipped in and out of May, her fingers played with it. May had a large cunt, and Elsie's little finger could slip in beside Charlie's cock.

Her cunt was on his backbone, and on that she frigged herself—he felt the warm love moisture much about the same time as he spent himself in May.

He didn't recollect the actual end, didn't recollect anything till a stream of daylight dazzled him into being, and he found himself alone—with a little note pinned on each side of his broad pillow.

Each read the same: 'Thanks *so* much.'

Only the handwriting and the signature were different. One 'Elsie'—the other 'May'.

Pauline the Prima Donna

Among the persons attending the rehearsal I noticed a stranger who immediately made a strong impression on me: a very handsome man, well dressed, with an intelligent face. When the tenor sang a false note, he leaped to the stage, took the score, and sang the passage with such passion and so much expression and taste that the whole cast was enraptured. I have never heard a voice his equal; it sent shivers of delight the length of my spine. Everyone applauded wildly and the tenor cried, 'After you, sir, it would be a profanation for me to continue!' And with that he ripped up the rest of his score.

I asked Monsieur de R. who he was and if he was Hungarian.

'You are asking me more than I can tell you,' he replied. 'His card carries the name Ferry. He could be Hungarian, English, Italian or Spanish, as well as French, German or Russian. He seems to speak all languages. I have not yet seen his papers, and the only thing I know is that he has just arrived from Vienna, that he is received at court there, that the English ambassador has recommended him to his *chargé d'affaires* for something or other, that he has dined with the manager of the royal theatre, and that everyone is happy to have him at dinner. I think that he is on some sort of diplomatic mission, and I know that he is living at the *Hotel de la Reine d'Angleterre*.'

Ferry remained to the end of the rehearsal and we were introduced. He was a perfect and gallant gentleman, and I had to watch myself closely when speaking with him.

I was always free in the evening when I had a long rehearsal in the afternoon or morning, and someone had recommended that I go often to the theatre in order to hear good Hungarian spoken. So that night I attended a performance accompanied by Madame de F. At the first intermission I had the pleasure of an unexpected visit from Ferry. He excused himself for coming to see me so quickly, but I begged him to stay. He paid me several compliments, saying he liked my voice very much, that I had good stage presence, that my costumes and makeup were excellent, etc., but he never spoke a word of love. He was simple and polite, never common and never importunate, and I resolved then and there to make a conquest of this man before the women of Budapest society got to him. I immediately brought all of my charm and coquetry into play, thinking to win him rapidly and, as he asked permission to pay me a visit soon, I thought that I had already won. I was soon to discover my error.

We finally did speak of love, but in a very general way. However much his eyes were eloquent, his tongue remained mute, and if his words left me in no doubt of how much I pleased him, he never so much as hinted at asking the slightest favour. When he pressed my hands upon arriving or leaving, he did it almost nonchalantly, without attaching the least bit of significance to it.

Finally, even so, I managed to steer the conversation to his past loves, and I asked him if he had made many conquests and if he had ever been seriously in love.

'I take the beautiful where I find it,' he replied. 'I believe that it would be an injustice to bind myself to a single individual and I think, in theory, that marriage is the most tyrannical institution in society. How can a man of honour dare to offer that which does not depend solely on his good will? Generally speaking, I believe that one should never promise anything to anyone, and you will never find a soul that can say to you truthfully that I have once promised him something. I do not even promise to come to a dinner when I have been invited; I content myself simply with acknowledging the invitation. I never gamble; chance is too great a power for me to give it the opportunity to defeat me. And that is why I never promise a woman to remain faithful to her. She must take me as I am if she takes me at all. If she is willing to share my heart with others, she will find plenty of room. That is the reason that I have never yet made a declaration of love to a woman; I always wait until she tells me simply and frankly that I please her enough so that she can no longer refuse me anything.'

'I imagine that you have already come across many such persons,' I said to him, 'but I cannot understand how you have been able to love them. It seems to me that a woman must be extremely imprudent to dare take the first steps in an affair, without waiting for the man to assume the initiative and make the overtures.'

'And why, may I ask?' he replied. 'Does not a man prefer a woman that loves him enough to dare to break all the laws of conventionality to one that simply plays a role? Women who demand the man's initiative are only going to give in at last in any case. A man infinitely prefers a woman who knows how to sacrifice her vanity to a woman who only knows how to be a coquette. Bitterness often pushes a man to revenge himself on a woman who has made him languish a long time, and when she finally cedes to him what he wishes, he will be unfaithful to her and leave her.'

'And those unfortunate young women that cede to the first attack of the man, do they also merit his vengeance?'

'I have never revenged myself but on coquettes, and I would certainly not like to seduce a young, innocent girl. I have never done it either, although God knows I've had the opportunities. Each woman that I have had has offered herself to me without my asking anyone to sacrifice her virginity. Each of them was free to choose, and they said to themselves, 'Should I prefer him who pursues me and who does not please me, or him who pleases me and says nothing?' And each of their choices fell upon me. They managed to free themselves from the foolish scruples that their mothers, aunts and other frustrated spinsters had taught them from childhood, and they played their game in the open. None of them ever regretted it, for each knew the risks she was running; I explained to each one that, though she could possibly become a mother, even so I would never marry her, that I loved other women as well as her, and that she might never see me again. Tell me, was I honest or not?'

I could not deny it, but I also told him I would never dare to make a declaration of love to a man.

'Then,' he said, 'you will never love a man. For love in a woman entails sacrifice, and I will never show the slightest favour to a woman that will not give me the proof of such a love.'

He had answered everything I had asked; I knew now that he would never make a declaration of love to me. However, it was evident that I pleased him. Why else did he visit me so often? He preferred to be in my company rather than go out for the evening. Nevertheless, I hesitated. I wanted to make the declaration he wished, but I wanted to do it in such a manner as to save myself as many blushes as possible, and I hoped to find a means during the carnival. I didn't know if he thought me experienced or not but, in any case, virginity obviously had no particular charm for him. What he would have liked would have been a virgin as corrupt as a Mesalina. Unfortunately, there are no such virgins.

I did not know if I ought to confide in someone and have them act as an intermediary. I finally talked to Anna. She told me that although Ferry had already succumbed to another woman, she would do everything possible to win him for me. Above all, however, she wanted to know if he were going to participate in the orgy which was to take place in the brothel.

Several days later she brought me the news that Ferry's mistress was the Countess O. Her chambermaid had overheard the initial conversation between the two. He had proposed exactly the same conditions to the countess, adding to the two that he had mentioned to me as being necessary—that the woman must make the overtures and that she must not count on his fidelity—a third: that each woman who gave herself to him must be completely nude. When a woman accorded everything to a man, he asserted, there was no reason for her not to reveal herself completely. The countess had accepted.

I do not know if I could abandon myself in that

fashion, even if I were to be in love. I am very liberal on that point; however, I cannot free myself from a certain prudishness which, innate or acquired, still dominates me. I have not yet learned whether this facet of my character is common to all women.

In the meantime, Anna told me that, though Ferry would undoubtedly participate in the orgy, as he had been invited by three women, he had not promised definitely, for it was against his principles.

The evening of the orgy approached rapidly. Anna, Rose and Nina helped me to finish my costume and try it on. It was made of a sky-blue silk, very heavy, with insertions of white gauze and brocaded gold flowers. My buttocks and, in front, my breasts and my belly, from the navel to three inches below my grotto of delight, were uncovered. On my feet I was wearing a pair of crimson velvet-tipped sandals. My collar was the ruffled lace one sees in portraits of Mary Stuart. The sleeves of my dress were elbow length and embroidered in gold. An Indian shawl, also in gold, was fastened about my waist and my hair was adorned with multicoloured marabou feathers.

I did not want to wear my own jewels, as they would have given away my identity, so I left them with a Jewess, who lent me some others. Besides this, I carried a staff with a gilded penis in erection on its tip, and wore a mask that covered my whole face except for the mouth and eyes. The colour of my hair was not unusual enough to betray me, although there were very few women who could claim locks as rich as mine. In all, my costume was in very good taste and quite original.

The 23rd of January, Anna and I went to the house on the Goldstickergasse, I wearing a heavy cloak over my attire. When we arrived, Anna left me in the vestibule and I was received by Resi Luft. Although the hall was already well filled and the orchestra playing, the first men I saw upon entering were Monsieur de F. and the baron. They were almost entirely nude, wearing only a sort of skimpy bathing suit in clinging silk, and they wore no masks. My entry, meanwhile, had created a sensation. I heard the women murmuring, 'There is the one that is going to beat us tonight! . . . My, she is pretty! . . . That one is made of sugar, and how I would love to eat some of it! . . .' And the men were even more excited. The most beautiful parts of my body—my breasts, my arms, my calves, my buttocks, and my sex—were all bare or scarcely veiled. I waited not a second, taking the opportunity to seek out Ferry immediately. I finally found him dancing with a woman dressed in white tulle scattered over with roses and lilies, for she was supposed to be a nymph. Her body was fairly well proportioned, but not as beautiful as mine. Another woman had her arm around Ferry's hips. She represented Venus, and the only articles she wore were a belt of gold, a few diamonds and a crown in her raven black hair. She held the great, erect sceptre of her partner in her hand, and I must admit that I have never seen as large nor as handsome a lance as his. It was of an extraordinary size, as red as the sandals that were the only clothing of its master, and it shone as if it had been dipped in oil. The rest of Ferry's body was a gleaming white, tinted here and there with pinks and roses. Not even an Apollo, a Belvedere or an Antinous could have been as handsome or as well proportioned as he, and I trembled at the sight of him. My eyes were so busy devouring him that I stopped involuntarily before the tableau of which he was the centre. His Venus had a very pretty body, very white, but her breasts were slightly pendulous, and her violet-lipped grotto was too open, too ravaged by love.

Suddenly Ferry's eyes found and rested on mine. He smiled very slightly and said, 'Very good. That is much the best method by which to take the initiative.' He then broke away from his women and came towards me, bent his head down to mine, and whispered my name in my ear. I blushed scarlet beneath my mask.

The orchestra, separated by a great screen from the revellers, broke into a waltz, Ferry took me by the waist, and we whirled into the maelstrom of couples. The contact of all those bodies, burning and brilliant, male and female, infatuated me. All the members of the men were fully erect and, during the dance, turning towards a common goal. Kisses bubbled everywhere, and an exquisite perfume began to float upwards from the closely clasped bodies. I was dizzy with joy. I felt Ferry's dagger touch me suddenly, butting its head like a maddened bull against my sex. I pressed myself against him, spreading my legs so that he could enter lower down, but he did not attempt it, asking me instead, 'Are you ever jealous?'

'No!' I responded quickly. 'I want to see you like Mars and Venus.'

He left me quickly and took Venus, who was dancing with another man. Meanwhile two of the girls of the house, Vladislava and Leonie, brought out a stool covered with red velvet and placed it in the middle of the room. Venus bent over it, leaning on it with her hands, and Ferry attacked her from the rear.

Vladislava and Leonie then knelt at the feet of the combatants, the first spreading Venus' lips, the other tickling Ferry's testicles. Ferry gave Venus such a riding that she was soon groaning in ecstasy; I was now feverishly stripping myself. I now stood entirely nude before him and asked, 'The mask too?'

'Keep it,' he said and, withdrawing his rod from the goddess, shooed her off with a smack on the behind so that I could take her place. My knees turned to rubber. Ferry then kneeled before me, tonguing me so masterfully that I thought I would surely discharge; finally he attacked me from the rear as he had my predecessor. I noticed then that his rod was the splendid rose colour of the symbol on the staff I had carried to the ball.

It was too much! Venus and another woman were sucking my breasts, a third was kissing me and thrusting her tongue between my lips to suck and bite, while Leonie was kneeling between my legs and tickling the base of my font with her tongue. My senses whirled, my breath rasped in my throat, and my whole body trembled; everywhere hips, thighs, arms and buttocks burned me, and from my font flowed a whirling stream like whipped cream, jetting into the mouth of Ferry, who drank it to the last drop. Then he leaped to his feet once more with a bound and drove his great sceptre into me to the root. All my nerves, which before had been distended, now knotted with desire; my temple of pleasure was on fire; the shaft of stone ravaged me like a knife. How that man could ride in the joust of love! Sometimes he completely withdrew his weapon, rubbed the head against my lips, then thrust it in again suddenly and violently. I could feel the tiny opening of my hymen attempting to absorb the enormous head of his mace; it held it tightly, as if in a vice, until he completely tore it violently open. He repeated this game several times, his movements accelerating and becoming more abandoned, while his rod expanded even more. He was no longer master of his desires, and he leaned heavily upon me. His fingers bruised my thighs, his mouth sank into my shoulder, and his tongue sucked the blood. Suddenly I felt his jet inundate me and overflow my sex.

I thought that I had lost the game, that all was over, but at once he began afresh, his weapon a prisoner in my cavern of joy, regaining its vigour little by little. He kept up the assault and I responded with ardour. The duel continued, but more carefully, more slowly, to the applause of the spectators, who had now formed a circle around us. Thrust followed thrust at regular intervals; I suddenly felt an electric shock that nearly paralyzed me—a great jet even more scalding than the first ripped through my body.

Once more he was to prove his strength to me, his love and his virility. The spectators became delirious when they saw him withdraw his sword from the scabbard for the third time and for the third time thrust it back in to renew the combat of love. They began to cry, 'All good things come in threes!' This time the game lasted a good quarter of an hour and they watched it to the end. Ferry was indefatigable, but the crisis had to arrive sooner or later and our joy was infinite. He inundated me with his sperm, carrying our passion to undreamed of heights. I was no longer standing on my own feet. Several of the girls of the house were supporting me, while from all sides, I felt nothing but nude flesh. Women were covering me with kisses and biting my nipples, while Ferry, still standing behind me, clasped me in his arms.

Finally they left us alone. Ferry clasped me once more and then offered me his arm to take me to another room. 'On the throne! On the throne!' cried several voices, for there had been erected at one end of the hall a sort of throne made of an ottoman covered with red velvet and surmounted with a canopy of purple. It was there that they wished to carry us in triumph, to indicate that we had won first place among all the combats of love. Ferry declined in my name, thanked them for the honour, and said that if it were permitted he would prefer to take a short rest. Thereupon the woman who was dressed as Venus took us into the banquet hall, but the table was not yet prepared.

'Isn't there a private room somewhere where my Titania (he called me thus, for he said that I was most beautiful of the beautiful) can rest quietly for a minute?'

'Resi Luft ought to have several,' replied Venus. 'I will tell her to ready one for you.' She disappeared and soon returned with our hostess. At sight of her, we burst into gales of laughter, for she had followed our example and was completely nude. She was old, enormously fat, and incredibly greasy, a perfect twin of that famous queen of the South Sea Islands, Nomahanna. Oh, those great reddish rolls of flesh and that timber forest beneath her belly! But somehow she proved appetizing yet, for I understand that she found several men to taste her charms and to let themselves be swallowed up in that sea of flesh.

She let us into a small room near the dance hall,

from where we could watch the progress of the bacchanal. There were several couples still dancing, but most of them preferred a more serious occupation. We could hear the murmur of voices, the sound of kisses, the panting of men, and the sighs of women. I was sitting on the knees of my lover, and becoming more and more excited by what I could see, when something hard and hot rose against my buttocks. I did not need to guess what it was.

'You are not ready to start again?' I asked him, covering his mouth with kisses.

'And why not, may I ask?' he said, laughing. 'But would you refuse if I shut the door and asked you to remove your mask? I want to be able to see the sensuality and the pleasure in your face.'

He was not the tyrant that I had thought. This despot of mine was as mild and caressing as a shepherd. I went to the door and shut it. Then I turned, took off my mask, and threw myself on the bed. I spread my thighs, pushed myself up on my elbows, and awaited my cavalier. He didn't hesitate a second before ramming home his lance, and this time there was no one to disturb us. I saw only him and he saw only me.

Can I possibly tell you what I felt? No, I think not. It will have to suffice to say that we drank three consecutive libations to the gods of love, and I simply cannot tell you the joy I felt at having these all by myself and in privacy. When the crisis approached, his eyes fixed themselves on mine and took on a savage expression of desire. We rolled breast to breast, stomach to stomach, arms and legs entwined like serpents. At the end, we lay side by side, his sceptre still inside my case, our eyes closed, resting and finally falling asleep. We lay in this ecstasy a good half-hour until the sound of the revels reaching their peak awakened us. I dressed hurriedly, forgetting my mask, which Ferry took and put on my face, and we reentered the hall.

The orgy had indeed reached its height. You could see nothing but groups of bodies, in every imaginable pose, made up of two, three, four and five persons.

There were two groups that were particularly complicated. One was composed of a man and six women. He was lying on his back on a plank across two chairs. He was running one girl through with his lance; another was sitting on his chest while he licked her grotto; his hands were tickling the fonts of two other girls; the remaining two were being invaded in their sensitive spots by his big toes. These last two were actually playing less; they were there only to complete the group and had to pretend to be satisfying themselves.

The other group was composed of Venus, who was stretched across one man who invaded her from the front, while another attacked her rear, an opening much smaller than the first. In her two hands she manipulated the organs of two other men. The fifth man, a giant from Rhodes, knelt on two chairs above the head of the first, who sucked his shaft of love. The climax was achieved at the same time among all six of them. It was undoubtedly the best group.

A third group was made up of two women and one man. One of the women was lying on her back, the other on the stomach of the first with her legs tightly wrapped around the hips of her partner. They were both spread voluptuously, biting and licking each other. The man dressed like Hercules, forced his lance first into one and then into the other, and I was curious to see how they would share his vital fluid when the time came. As it turned out, it was a reasonable and just division; neither received more than the other. When the crisis struck he did not lose his head, but doled the nectar out equally. The one on the bottom received the first.

Every man and woman at this ball took part in the activities. No one remained a wallflower. Everyone was a combatant at least twice, and Ferry among the men and I among the women were in the best form.

Venus, the Countess Bella, and I were the only women who had so far remained masked. Later on I learned that Venus was a woman famous for her affairs and I discovered her identity. She never, however, removed her mask. The Countess Bella was a veritable fury, a female demon. She cried in a loud voice, 'Look! Look! Don't you know that I am a whore, a real whore!' She then made a tour of all the ladies of the house, giving them candy, fruit or champagne. At the table, she drank a full tumbler of brandy that a man had poured for her and rolled dead-drunk onto the floor. Resi Luft dragged her into a room and locked the door, while Bella tried to break it down. Finally she went fast asleep. Later, two of the whores went to see if she were still sleeping and found her flowing from every opening like a leaky barrel. They put her on a bed and she slept until four the next afternoon.

The supper was in every way worthy of the orgy. Several persons slept on the table, and there were not more than two men besides Ferry who were capable of comporting themselves decently. The others were left standing by, hanging their heads sadly. Finally the prizes were distributed. Ferry was proclaimed the king, followed by one who had played the harmonica very well, and a third who had given out a lot of candy. My chief rival, the Princess O, whom I had found in Ferry's company, had finished him off very well. I tried to get him to drink until he was drunk, thinking that it was a chance of reviving him, but he refused. However, he did down one more glass of brandy before the orgy terminated at four o'clock in the morning.

Ferry and I, Venus and several other women went home. The rest were drunk and passed the remainder of the night at Resi Luft's.

On the whole, I noticed that the girls of our hostess conducted themselves better than the other women. They had been asked to take part in the ball by the men beforehand and all continued into the bacchanal that followed except Leonie. However, it was said that she was actually a member of the nobility, and that she had left her parents, members of an old Viennese family, to come directly to Resi Luft and practise her adopted *métier*.

Ferry accompanied me to my apartment, where Rose was still up awaiting me. She did not go to bed until I finally asked her to, and need I tell you that for Ferry, who was himself again, and I, the war of love was not yet over for that night?

I was splitting my pleasure, during those days in Budapest, with two persons, Ferry and Rose. The former was my declared lover while the latter served to vary my excitements.

One day Ferry surprised me by saying that until he had met me he had never known real love, that his long-held principles were no longer as solid as they once had been, and that he could now admit his fidelity. If I wished, he added, he would now consent to marry me. Despite the allure of such a proposition, I refused and was forced to refuse many times again when he continued to put the proposition before me. I was too afraid of killing our love by attaching other bonds to it, for I firmly believe that both the church and the state have made marriage a tomb for love. The memory of the happy life of my parents did not serve to reassure me, for I felt that that had been pure chance. Very simply, I loved and the secret of our pleasures only served to augment my love. Ferry appreciated and finally adopted my views.

I abandoned myself completely to love. I loved no one but Ferry and, thanks to his prudence, no one suspected our relations and my reputation did not suffer in the slightest.

Rose, however, had much more to complain of. Ferry took no notice of her to speak of, and I rarely had a night free to spend with her. Realizing this, and since I was not a victim of any kind of jealousy, I asked myself if it would not be wise to push her into the arms of Ferry also. The taking of her virginity with the aid of my rubber instrument that night had not been completely successful, for the membrane had resumed its former position and she was once more as good as new. You are probably going to say this is impossible, but I assure you that several months after the episode with Anna and Nina I attempted to insert my finger into her cavern and found my way blocked. I made her lie down on the couch and examined her grotto very carefully under a lamp. She spread her legs and I saw an entry that was completely round, with a little partition that was quite hard and completely inelastic. It reminded me of the presentation of a virgin at the panopticum on St. Joseph's Square near the fair of Budapest . . . I am not religious and I am only telling you what I saw.

I asked Rose if she would like to have a lover like Ferry, and she replied that when she had me she did not want any man. She said that if she had to sacrifice her virginity to a man she would be doing it only for my pleasure. Ferry did not seem to her any more desirable than any other man she had known.

Very few women know the pleasure of watching the combats of another couple and very few men feel anything but scorn for a woman who gives herself to another man before their eyes. Ferry and I were exceptions.

Ferry had often asked me to give myself up to another man before his eyes, but I had always refused, thinking that he wanted to quit me and that he was only looking for an excuse. I had not yet begun to believe that it was only pleasure he was after. However, he told me of many examples of the same thing, citing in history the cases of Gatta and Melatta, the Venetian heroes who never made love to their wives until they had abandoned themselves to another man. Finally I was convinced, and we decided that Ferry should teach the art of love to Rose and that afterwards I would do the same with a young man.

I had a great deal of difficulty in convincing Rose that she should take part. She threw herself into my arms, crying and saying that I no longer loved her, and I had to try to prove the opposite. I kissed and sucked her front, I bit the nipples on her breasts, I excited her so that she panted with desire. Then Ferry helped me to strip her and soon she was nude before us. Ferry kissed her tenderly and passionately, stroking her foaming grotto with his shaft of love until finally the moment arrived. He picked her up and carried her to the bed where he placed several pillows beneath her behind. She spread her legs involuntarily and he kneeled between them. The little fake was trembling in all her limbs, but she had her eyes closed so that we should not see how much she really wanted the pleasure that was about to come. I kneeled on another pillow so that her head was underneath my stomach. She immediately pressed me with her left hand while her right held tightly to Ferry, to whom I had turned my stern. When Ferry finally broke through Rose's membrane she bit me violently. Even this pain was wonderful. Neither Rose nor I could prevent from crying out in ecstasy; Ferry alone was silent.

Rose was so violent in her pleasure that Ferry could hardly stay aboard her. She bucked, groaned, then cried out passionately or cooed like a dove. We lay there, one on top of the other, one within the other, and our burning bodies smoked in the bed. I forced my nose deep into Rose's armpit and lay there, drunker than if I had been drinking all evening. Our ecstasy was infinite.

Little by little we recovered and left the soaked bed. Ferry advised us to take a bath at once, which we did. In Budapest, I had made a hot bath a daily luxury, for I found that it always revived me immediately, no matter how fatigued I was by either love or work, and it did no less for us this time.

Ferry was a master of love. He knew every means for increasing and renewing pleasure. And this time he was no less imaginative. When Rose and I got out of the tub and began to dry ourselves, he stopped us and told us instead to rub soap and oil over our bodies. This we did, and our bodies became as slippery as those of two eels. Then he had me lean over the bathtub while he hoisted Rose to his shoulders. In this position, with her facing him, he attacked me from the rear, not through the ordinary tunnel, but through a neighbouring one that up until then had been virgin to me. He had smeared it well with oil, making his entry much easier. However, it did hurt a little.

While he was thus occupied, he put his arms around me and forced his fingers in through my cavern and I could feel his hands inside me almost reaching his shaft. Only a thin layer of skin seemed to separate them. Sensuality was, at that point, much stronger than pain and I was completely ravished by desire. In the meantime, Rose slipped onto my shoulders so that her temple of love was now before my mouth. The game was exquisite and we all came at the same time. However, Ferry would have finished his play much sooner than either Rose or I if he had not kept his head. For he was forced to stop and remove his arrow from my quiver several times in order to remain master of himself. Each time that he returned to the assault a sharp pain which quickly turned to a quenching sensuality filled me. It was thus that he attacked five or six times before we were all reduced to intoxication. Rose's fountain overflowed its banks. In the meantime the flow from Ferry's weapon inundated my interior and my own source sprang forth.

I can never remember having had an experience like that again. It was undoubtedly the height of my sensuality and I will never be able to forget that game in my life. We finally parted and went to Rose's bed to sleep, for mine was still afloat. We lay down, Ferry in the middle and the two of us pressing on him from both sides.

Ever since that night I have never been able to understand jealousy in women. It no longer seems to me reasonable and natural that these things do not happen more frequently in our civilized countries, for I am convinced that copulation and desire have for their object, not the perpetuation of the species, but simply the experiences of sensuality.

The very next day Ferry reminded me of my promise and assured me that if I carried it out no one should ever know. He told me to accompany him on a short trip.

It was spring and the weather was magnificent. Ferry told me we would leave Budapest on the day after the next, and he spent the intervening twenty-four hours entirely with me.

We left the city on a Sunday at two o'clock in the morning. Taking Ferry's private carriage instead of a train or boat, we travelled the rest of the night until we reached Nessmely around eight in the morning. There we left the main highway, crossed Igmand, and arrived at around noon in the famous forest of Bakony. At an inn in the middle of the forest we found a table already prepared for us. There were several rather sinister and evil looking men about, and I thought that they were perhaps robbers. Ferry talked with them a few moments in Hungarian and I asked him worriedly what they were up to. He told me that they were just some poor devils that lived in the wood, and that I had nothing to fear. In the afternoon, after we had eaten, we climbed back into our coach, this time preceded by five horsemen.

We no longer went as fast as we had, for the road was very bad and narrow. Finally we arrived at the densest part of the forest and once more alit from our carriage. We walked the rest of the way and the coach was driven to a building which I could barely see through the trees and which looked like an inn. The horsemen preceded us, parting the branches for our passage, and we finally reached a beautiful glade with a large and deep stream. We rested there and ate, and an hour later, two men appeared. One was about thirty-four or thirty-five and was built like a Hercules. His face was savage but very regular, almost handsome. The other, scarcely twenty, was as beautiful as Adonis. Ferry presented the two men and told me I would now taste the thrills of love with them, that I had nothing to fear, and that neither knew who I was nor had the slightest relation with the outside world.

The Hercules immediately stripped, but the young man blushed and hesitated. Ferry gave him a sharp command and he followed suit. I undressed slowly and Ferry told me that I should abandon myself completely, because the more passionate I was the more pleasure he would take in the sight. However, knowing his thoughts, I resolved to be as dissolute as possible. I called the two men and took them by their lances. The little mushroom of the young man immediately became a branch of oak that reached all the way up to his navel. The giant's sword had unsheathed itself as soon as I had undressed. I took the young man's weapon and started to tickle the end of it but as soon as I touched it I received the full flow of his burning discharge. In the meantime, the giant lifted me by my buttocks until my behind was touching his stomach and, without my guiding him, thrust his lance straight into my shell. I thought he would penetrate right up to my throat, his weapon was so long. His blows fell slowly, measuredly and powerfully, and I thought at each shock that I would swoon. However, I never loosened my grasp on the young man's shaft and it soon grew hard and strong once more.

'Is it good?' Ferry asked me. He was not yet undressed himself.

I could only reply to his answer with my eyes. I almost fainted with delight and my lock gates began to open wide until they finally released my precious nectar, flooding the giant's great shaft. However, he continued without tiring, and worked a good half hour before he began to feel his crisis approach.

'Don't give her any children!' cried Ferry, laughing.

'Don't worry! Where I'm going to end up you'll never find a baby growing!'

And with that, he removed his redoubtable staff from my shell and I thought I would die from pain when he forced it into the neighbouring hole. He gave only two thrusts when the juice from his loins flowed in a jet that lasted at least a full minute. It repaid him well for his long labour and finally he withdrew his dart. He had so skinned me that I could not at all sit down and scarcely walk. He carried me to the stream and washed my wound with his fingers, thereby soothing my pain, but I still could not walk a step. I was very sorry not to have accorded the young man more pleasure, but I had solaced him twice.

I remained about an hour in the water, then the

giant took me in his arms and three men helped him dress me. They finally took me into the house where Ferry put me to bed.

Can I describe to you vividly enough the three days that I passed in that forest? I changed lovers every day and even more often than that, for there were nine brigands. And the third day we celebrated with a great orgy with the peasants from nearby. Agrippina would have envied our saturnalias. These peasants were as skilful and adroit as the aristocrats of Budapest.

I had plenty of time to rest up during the rest of my vacation and Rose alone accompanied me. I left Ferry after many tender farewells, but it was necessary, for many more debauches would have surely killed me.

A Man with a Maid

'I was very angry with my maid this morning and it would have delighted me to have spanked her severely. Now, would such delight arise from satisfied revenge or from being cruel?'

'Undoubtedly from being cruel,' I replied, 'the infliction of the punishment is what would have given you the pleasure, and behind it would come the feeling that you were revenging yourself. Here's another instance—you women delight in saying nasty cutting things to each other in the politest of ways; why? Not from revenge, but from the satisfaction afforded by the shot going home. If you had given your maid this morning a box on the ears you would have satisfied your revenge without any pleasure whatever; but if I had been there and held your maid down while you spanked her bottom, your pleasure would have arisen from the infliction of the punishment. Do you follow me, dear?'

'Yes, I see it now,' Alice replied, then added archly: 'I wish you had been there, Jack! it would have done her a lot of good!'

'I sometimes wonder why you keep her on,' I said musingly. 'She's a pert minx and at times must be very aggravating. Let me see—what's her name?'

'Fanny.'

'Yes, of course—a case of 'pretty Fanny's way,' for she certainly is a pretty girl and a well-made one. My dear, if you want to do bottom slapping, you won't easily find a better subject, only I think she will be more than you can manage single-handed, and it may come to her slapping your bottom, my love!'

Alice laughed. 'Fanny is a most perfect maid, a real treasure, or I would not keep her on—for as you say, she is too much for me. She's very strong and very high-spirited, but wants taming badly.'

'Bring her some afternoon, and we'll tame her between us!' I suggested seemingly carelessly.

Alice started, raised herself on her elbows and regarded me questioningly. I noticed a hard glitter in her eyes, then she caught her breath, coloured, then exclaimed softly: 'Oh, Jack, how lovely it would be!'

I had succeeded! Alice had succumbed to the sudden temptation! For the second time her strain of lascivious sexuality had conquered.

'Shall we try?' I asked with a smile, secretly delighted at her unconcealed eagerness and noting how her eyes now were brimming over with lust and how her lovely breasts were heaving with her excitement.

'Yes! Yes! Jack!' she exclaimed feverishly, 'but how can it be managed?'

'There shouldn't be much trouble,' I replied. 'Take her out with you shopping some afternoon close by here, then say you want just to pop in to see me about something. En route tell her about this room, how it's sound-proof, it will interest her and she will at the same time learn information that will come in useful later on. Once in here follow my lead. I suppose you would like to have a go at her?'

'Oh! Jack!' exclaimed Alice, her eyes sparkling with eagerness, 'will you fasten her down as you did me?'

I nodded.

'Yes! Yes! let me have a turn at her!' she replied

vivaciously. Then after a pause she looked queerly at me and added, 'and will you . . . ? at the same moment significantly squeezing my prick.

'I think so—unless of course you would rather I didn't, dear,' I replied with a laugh; 'I suppose you have no idea whether she is a virgin or not?'

'I can't say!' Alice replied, blushing a little. 'I've always fancied she was and have treated her as such.'

'And what sort of treatment is that?' I queried mischievously, and was proceeding to cross-question Alice when she stopped me by putting her hand over my mouth.

'Well, we'll soon find out when we get her here,' I remarked philosophically, much to her amusement.

Next afternoon, after seeing that everything was in working order in the Snuggery, I threw open both doors as if carelessly, and taking off my coat as if not expecting any visitors, I proceeded to potter about the room, keep a vigilant eye on the stairs. Before long I heard footsteps on the landing, but pretended not to know that any one was there till Alice tapped merrily on the door saying: 'May we come in, Jack?'

'Good Heavens, Alice?' I exclaimed in pretended surprise as I struggled hurriedly to get into my coat—'come in! how do you do? where have you dropped from?'

'We've been shopping—this is my maid, Jack'—I bowed and smiled, receiving in return from Fanny a distinctly pert and not too respectful nod—'and as we were close by, I thought I would take the chance of finding you in and take away that enlargement if it is ready.'

By this time I had struggled into my coat: 'It's

quite ready,' I replied. 'I'll go and get it, and I don't know why those doors should stand so unblushingly open,' I added with a laugh.

Having closed them, noiselessly locking them, I disappeared into the alcove I used for myself, and pretended to search for the enlargement—my real object being to give Alice a chance of letting Fanny know the nature of the room. Instinctively she divined my idea, and I heard her say: 'This is the room I was telling you about. Fanny—look at the double doors, the padded walls, the rings, the pillars, the hanging pulley straps! Isn't it queer?'

Fanny looked about her with evident interest: 'It *is* a funny room, Miss! And what are those little places for?' pointing to the two alcoves.

'We do not know, Fanny,' Alice replied, 'Mr Jack uses them for his photographic work now.'

As she spoke, I emerged with a large print which was to represent the supposed enlargement, and gave it to Alice who at once proceeded to closely examine it.

I saw that Fanny's eyes were wandering all over the room, and I moved over to her: 'A strange room Fanny eh?' I remarked. 'Is it not still; no sound from outside can get in, and no noise from inside can get out! That's a fact, we've tested it thoroughly!'

'Lor', Mr Jack!' she replied in her forward familiar way, turning her eyes on me in a most audacious and bold way, then resuming her survey of the room.

While she was doing so, I hastily inspected her. She was a distinctly pretty girl tall, slenderly but strongly built, with an exquisitely well-developed figure. A slightly turned-up nose and dark flashing eyes gave her face a saucy look which her free style of moving accentuated, while her dark hair and rich colouring indicated a warm-blooded and passionate temperament. I easily could understand that Alice with her gentle ways was no match for Fanny; and I fancied that I should have my work cut out for me before I got her arms fastened to the pulley ropes.

Alice now moved towards us, print in hand: 'Thanks awfully, Jack, it's lovely!' and she began to roll it up. 'Now, Fanny, we must be off!'

'Don't bother about the print, I'll send it after you,' I said. 'And where are you off to now?'

'Nowhere in particular,' she replied, 'we'll look at the shops and the people. Good-bye, Jack!'

'One moment,' I interposed. 'You were talking the other day about some perfection of a lady's maid that you didn't want to lose—' (Fanny smiled complacently)'—but whose tantrums and ill tempers were getting more than you could stand.' (Fanny here began to look angry.) 'Somebody suggested that you should give her a good spanking—' (Fanny assumed a contemptuous air)'—or if you couldn't manage it yourself you should get someone to do it for you!' (Fanny here glared at me.) 'Is this the young lady?'

Alice nodded, with a curious glance at Fanny, who was now evidently getting into one of her passions.

'Well, as you've nothing to do this afternoon, and she happens to be here, and this room is so eminently suitable for the purpose, shall I take the young woman in hand for you and teach her a lesson?'

Before Alice could reply, Fanny with a startled exclamation darted to the door, evidently bent on escape, but in spite of her vigorous twists of the handle and shakings, the door refused to open, for the simple reason that unnoticed by her I had locked it! Instantly divining that she was a prisoner, she turned hurriedly round to watch our movements, but she was too late! With a quickness learnt on the football field, I was onto her and pinned her arms to her sides in a grip that she could not break out of despite her frantic struggles: 'Let me go! . . . let me go, Mr Jack!' she screamed; I simply chuckled as I knew I had her safe now! I had to exert all my strength and skill for she was extraordinarily strong and her furious rage added to her power; but in spite of her desperate resistance, I forced her to the hanging pulleys where Alice was eagerly waiting for us. With astonishing quickness she made fast the ropes to Fanny's wrists and set the machinery going—and in a few seconds the surprised girl found herself standing erect with her arms dragged up taut over her head!

'Well done, Jack!' exclaimed Alice, as she delightedly surveyed the still struggling Fanny! The latter was indeed a lovely subject of contemplation, as with heaving bosom, flushed cheeks, and eyes that sparkled with rage, she stood panting, endeavouring to get back her breath, while her agitated fingers vainly strove to get her wrists free from the pulley ropes. We watched her in victorious silence, waiting for the outbursts of wrathful fury which we felt would come as soon as she was able to speak!

It soon came! 'How dare you, Mr Jack!' Fanny burst out as she flashed her great piercing eyes at us, her whole body trembling with anger; 'How dare you treat me like this! Let me loose at once, or as sure as I am alive, I'll have the law on you and also on that mealy-mouthed smooth-faced demure hypocrite that calls herself my mistress indeed!—who looks on while a poor girl is vilely treated and won't raise a finger to help her! Let me go at once, Mr Jack! and I'll promise to say and do nothing; but my God!—' (here her voice became shrill with overpowering rage)—my God! if you don't, I'll make it hot for the pair of you when I get out!' And she glared at us in her impotent fury.

'Your Mistress has asked me to give you a lesson, Fanny,' I replied calmly, 'and I'm going to do so! The sooner you recognize how helpless you really are, and will submit yourself to us, the sooner it will be over; but if you are foolish enough to resist, you'll have a long doing and a bad time! Now, if I let you loose, will you take your clothes off quietly?'

'My God! no!' she cried indignantly, but in spite of herself she blushed vividly!

'Then we'll take them off for you!' was my cool reply. 'Come along, Alice, you understand girl's clothes, you undo them and I'll get them off somehow!'

Quickly Alice sprang up, trembling with excitement, and together we approached Fanny, who shrieked defiance and threats at us in her impotent fury as she struggled desperately to get free. But as soon as she felt Alice's fingers unfastening her garments, her rage changed to horrible apprehension: and as one by one they slipped off her, she began to realize how helpless she was! 'Don't, Miss!' she ejaculated pitifully. 'My God! Stop her, Sir!' she pleaded, the use of these more respectful terms of address sufficiently proclaiming her changed attitude. But we were obdurate, and soon Fanny stood with only her chemise and undervest left on her, her shoes and stockings having been dragged off her at the special request of Alice, whose uncontrolled enjoyment of the work of stripping her maid was delicious to witness.

She now took command of operations. Pointing to a chair just in front of Fanny she exclaimed: 'Sit there, Jack, and watch Fanny as I take off her last garments.'

'For God's sake, Miss, don't strip me naked!' shrieked Fanny, who seemed to expect that she would be left in her chemise and to whom the sudden intimation that she was to be exposed naked came with an appalling shock! 'Oh, Sir! For God's sake, stop her!' she cried, appealing to me as she saw me take my seat right in front of her and felt Alice's fingers begin to undo the shoulder-strap fastenings which alone kept her scanty garments on her. 'Miss Alice! ... Miss Alice! don't! ... for God's sake, don't,' she screamed, in a fresh access of dismay as she felt her vest slip down her body to her feet and knew now her only covering was about to follow. In despair she tugged frantically at the ropes which made her arms so absolutely helpless, her agitated quivering fingers betraying her mental agony!

'Steady, Fanny, steady!' exclaimed Alice to her struggling maid as she proceeded to unfasten the chemise, her eyes gleaming with lustful cruelty: 'Now, Jack!' she said warningly, then let go, stepping back a pace herself the better to observe the effect! Down swept the chemise, and Fanny stood stark naked!!

'Oh! oh!' she wailed, crimson with shame, her face hidden on her bosom which now was wildly heaving in agitation. It was a wonderful spectacle!—in the foreground Fanny, naked, helpless, in an agony of shame—in the background but close to her was Alice exquisitely costumed and hatted, gloating over the sight of her maid's absolute nudity, her eyes intently fixed on the gloriously luscious curves of Fanny's hips, haunches, and bottom!

I managed to catch her eye and motioned to her to come and sit on my knee that we might in each other's close company study her maid's naked charms so reluctantly being exhibited to us. With one long last look she obeyed my summons. As she seated herself on my knees she threw her arms around my neck and kissed me rapturously whispering: 'Jack! Isn't she delicious!!' I nodded smilingly, then in turn muttered in her ear: 'And how do you like the game, dear?'

Alice blushed divinely: a strange languishing voluptuous half-wanton half-cruel look came into her eyes. Placing her lips carefully on mine she gave me three long-drawn kisses, the significance of which I could not possibly misunderstand, then whispered almost hoarsely: 'Jack, let me do all the . . . torturing and be content this time, with . . . fucking Fanny . . . and me too, darling!'

'She's your maid, and so-to-speak your property, dear,' I replied softly, 'so arrange matters just as you like: I'll leave it all to you and won't interfere unless you want me to do anything.'

She kissed me gratefully, then turned her eyes on Fanny, who during this whispered colloquy had been standing trembling her face still hidden from us, her legs pressed closely against each other as if to shield as much as possible her cunt from our sight.

I saw Alice's eyes wander over Fanny's naked body with evident pleasure, dwelling first on her magnificent lines and curves, then on her lovely breasts, and finally on the mass of dark curling moss-like hair that covered her cunt. She was a most deliciously voluptuous girl, one calculated to excite Alice to the utmost pitch of lust of which she was capable, and while secretly regretting that my share in the process of taming Fanny was to be somewhat restricted, I felt that I would enjoy the rare opportunity of seeing how a girl, hitherto chaste and well-regulated, would yield to her sexual instincts and passions when she had placed at her absolute disposal one of her own sex in a state of absolute nakedness!

Presently Alice whispered to me: 'Jack, I'm going to feel her!' I smiled and nodded. Fanny must have heard her, for as Alice rose, she for the first time raised her head and cried affrightedly: 'No, Miss, please, Miss, don't touch me!' and again she vainly strained at her fastenings, her face quivering and flushed with shame. But disregarding her maid's piteous entreaties, Alice passed behind her, then kneeling down began to stroke Fanny's bottom, a hand to each cheek!

'Don't, Miss!' yelled Fanny, arching herself outwards and away from Alice, and thereby unconsciously throwing the region of her cunt into greater prominence! But with a smile of cruel gratification, Alice continued her sweet occupation, sometimes squeezing, sometimes pinching Fanny's glorious half-moons, now and then extending her excursions over Fanny's round plump thighs, once indeed letting her hands creep up them till I really thought (and so did Fanny from the way she screamed and wriggled) that she was about to feel Fanny's cunt!

Suddenly Alice rose, rushed to me, and kissing me ardently whispered excitedly: 'Oh, Jack! she's just lovely! such flesh, such a skin! I've never felt a girl before, I've never touched any girl's breasts or . . . cunt . . . except of course my own,' she added archly, 'and I'm wild at the idea of handling Fanny. Watch me carefully, darling, and if I don't do it properly, tell me!' And back to Fanny she rushed, evidently in a state of intense eroticism!

This time Alice didn't kneel, but placed herself close behind Fanny (her dress in fact touching her) then suddenly she threw her arms around Fanny's body and seized her breasts: 'Miss Alice! . . . don't!' shrieked Fanny, struggling desperately, her flushed face betraying her agitation. 'Oh! how lovely! . . . how delicious! . . . how sweet! . . .' cried Alice, wild with delight and sexual excitement as she squeezed and played with Fanny's voluptuous breasts! Her head with its exquisite hat was just visible over Fanny's right shoulder, while her dainty dress showed on each side of the struggling agitated girl, throwing into bold relief her glorious shape and accentuating in the most piquant way Fanny's stark nakedness! Entranced, I gazed at the voluptuous spectacle, my prick struggling to break through the fly of my trousers! Fanny had now ceased her cries and was enduring in silence, broken only by her involuntary 'Oh's,' the violation of her breasts by Alice, whose little hands could scarcely grasp the luscious morsels of Fanny's flesh that they were so subtly torturing, but which nevertheless succeeded in squeezing and compressing them and generally in playing with them till the poor girl gasped in her shame and agony: 'Oh! Miss Alice! . . . Miss Alice! . . . stop! . . . stop!' her head falling forward in her extreme agitation.

With a smile of intense satisfaction, Alice suspended her torturing operations and gently stroked and soothed Fanny's breasts till the more regular breathing of the latter indicated that she had in a great degree regained her self-control. Then her expression changed. A cruel hungry light came into her eyes as she smiled wickedly and meaningly at me, then I saw her hands quit Fanny's breasts and glide over Fanny's stomach till they arrived at Fanny's cunt!

Fanny shrieked as if she had been stung: 'Miss Alice! . . . Miss Alice! . . . don't! don't touch me there! . . . oh! . . . oh! my God, Miss Alice! . . . oh! Miss Alice! take your hands away! . . .' at the same time twisting and writhing in a perfectly wonderful way in her frantic endeavours to escape from her mistress's hands, the fingers of which were now hidden in her cunt's mossy covering as they inquisitively travelled all over her Mont Venus and along the lips of the orifice itself. For some little time they contented themselves with feeling and pressing and toying caressingly with Fanny's cunt, then I saw one hand pause while the first finger of the other gently began to work its way between the pink lips I could just distinguish and disappear into the sweet cleft. 'Don't, Miss!' yelled Fanny, her agonized face now scarlet! While in her distress she desperately endeavoured to defend her cunt by throwing her legs in turn across her groin, to Alice's delight—her tell-tale face proclaiming the intense pleasure she was tasting in thus making her maid undergo such horrible torture!

Presently I noted an unmistakeable look of surprise in her eyes; her lips parted as if in astonishment, while her hand seemed to redouble its attack on Fanny's cunt, then she exclaimed: 'Why Fanny? What's this?

'Oh! Don't tell Mr Jack, Miss!' shrieked Fanny, letting her legs drop as she could no longer endure the whole weight of her struggling body on her slender wrists, 'don't let him know!'

My curiosity was naturally aroused and intently I watched the movements of Alice's hand which the fall of Fanny's legs brought again into full view. Her forefinger was buried up to the knuckle in her maid's cunt! The mystery was explained, Fanny was not a virgin!

Alice seemed staggered by her discovery. Abruptly she quitted Fanny, rushed to me, threw herself on my knees, then flinging her arms round my neck she whispered excitedly in my ear: 'Jack! she's been . . . had by someone . . . my finger went right in!'

'So I noticed, darling!' I replied quietly as I kissed her flushed cheek. 'I think you'd better let her rest a bit now, her arms will be getting numb from being kept over her head; let's fasten her to that pillar by passing her arms round it and shackling her wrists together. She can then rest a bit; and while she is recovering from her struggles hadn't you better . . . slip your clothes off also—for your eyes hint that you will want . . . something before long!'

Alice blushed prettily, then whispered as she kissed me ardently. 'I'd like . . . something now, darling!' Then she ran away to her dressing room.

Left alone with Fanny, I proceeded to transfer her from the pulley to the pillar; it was not a difficult task, as her arms were too numb (as I expected) to be of much use to her and she seemed stupified at our discovery that her maidenhead no longer existed. Soon I had her firmly fastened with her back pressing against the pillar. This new position had two great advantages: she could no longer hide her face from us and the backwards pull of her arms threw her breasts out. She glanced timidly at me as I stood admiring her luscious nakedness, and waiting for Alice's return.

After a short pause she whispered: 'Oh! Mr Jack! let me go! . . . I'll come to you whenever you wish . . . and let you do what you like . . . but . . . I'm afraid of Miss Alice today . . . she seems so strange! . . . oh! my God! she's naked!' she screamed as genuine alarm as Alice came out of her toilet room with only her shoes and stockings on, and her large matinee hat, a most coquettishly piquantly indecent object! Poor Fanny went red at the sight of her mistress and didn't know where to look as Alice came dancing along, her eyes noting with evident approval the position into which I had placed her maid.

'Mes compliments, mademoiselle!' I said with a low bow as she came up.

She smiled and blushed, but was too intent on Fanny to joke with me. 'That's lovely, Jack!' she exclaimed after a careful inspection of her now trembling maid. 'I like that much better, Jack.' Then catching me by the elbow, she pushed me towards my alcove saying: 'We both will want you presently, Jack!' Looking roguishly at me: 'So get ready! But tell me first, where are the feathers?

'Oh, that's your game!' I replied with a laugh. She nodded, colouring slightly, and I told her where she would find them.

I had a peep-hole in my alcove through which I could see all that passed in the room, and being curious to watch the two girls, I placed myself by it as I slowly undressed myself.

Having found the feathers, Alice placed the box near her, then, going right up to Fanny, she took hold of her own breasts with her hands, raised them till they were level with Fanny's, then leaning on Fanny so that their stomachs were in close contact, she directed her breasts against Fanny's, gently rubbing her nipples against Fanny's while she looked intently into Fanny's eyes! It was a most curious sight! The girl's naked bodies were touching from their ankles to their breasts their cunts were so close to each other that their hairs formed one mass, while their faces were so near to each other that the brim of Alice's matinee hat projected over Fanny's forehead!

Not a word was said! For about half a minute Alice continued to rub her breasts gently against Fanny's with her eyes fixed on Fanny's downcast face, then suddenly I saw both naked bodies quiver, and then Fanny raised her head and for the first time responded to Alice's glance, her colour coming and going! At the same moment, a languorous voluptuous smile swept over Alice's face, and gently she kissed Fanny, who flushed rosy red but as far as I could see did not respond.

'Won't you . . . love me, Fanny?' I heard Alice say softly but with a curious strained voice! Immediately I understood the position. Alice was lusting after Fanny! I was delighted! It was clear that Fanny had not yet reciprocated Alice's passion, and I determined that Alice should have every opportunity of satisfying her lust on Fanny's naked helpless body, till the latter was converted to Tribadism with Alice as the object.

'Won't you . . . love me, Fanny?' again asked Alice softly, now supplementing the play of her breasts against Fanny's by insinuating and significant pressings of her stomach against Fanny's, again kissing the latter sweetly. But Fanny made no response, and Alice's eyes grew hard with a steely cruel glitter which boded badly for Fanny!

Quitting Fanny, Alice went straight to the box of

feathers, picked out one, and returned to Fanny, feather in hand. The sight of her moving about thus, her breasts dancing, her hips swaying, her cunt and bottom in full view, her nakedness intensified by her piquant costume of hat, shoes and stockings, was enough to galvanize a corpse: it set my blood boiling with lust and I could hardly refrain from rushing out and compelling her to let me quench my fires in her! I, however, did resist the temptation, and rapidly undressed to my shoes and socks so as to be ready to take advantage of any chance that either of the girls might offer; but I remained in my alcove with my eye to the peep-hole as I was curious to witness the denouement of this strangely voluptuous scene, which Alice evidently wished to play single-handed.

No sooner did Fanny catch sight of the feather than she screamed: 'No! . . . no! Miss Alice! . . . don't tickle me!' at the same time striving frantically to break the straps that linked together her wrists and her ankles. But my tackle was too strong! Alice meanwhile had caught up a cushion which she placed at Fanny's feet and right in front of her, she knelt on it, rested her luscious bottom on her heels, and having settled herself down comfortably she, with a smile in which cruelty and malice were strangely blended, gloatingly contemplated for a moment her maid's naked and agitated body, then slowly and deliberately applied the tip of the feather to Fanny's cunt!

'Oh, my God! Miss Alice, don't!' yelled Fanny, writhing in delicious contortions in her desperate endeavours to dodge the feather. 'Don't, Miss!' she shrieked, as Alice, keenly enjoying her maid's distress and her vain efforts to avoid the torture, proceeded delightedly to pass the feather lightly along the sensitive lips of Fanny's cunt and finally set to work to tickle Fanny's clitoris, thereby sending her so nearly into hysterical convulsions that I felt it time I interposed.

As I emerged from my alcove Alice caught sight of me and dropped her hand as she turned towards me, her eyes sparkling with lascivious delight! 'Oh, Jack! did you see her?' she cried excitedly.

'I heard her, dear!' I replied ambiguously, 'and began to wonder whether you were killing her, so came out to see.'

'Not a bit of it!' she cried, hugely pleased, 'I'm going to give her another turn!' a declaration that produced from Fanny the most pitiful pleadings which however seemed only to increase Alice's cruel satisfaction, and she was proceeding to be as good as her word when I stopped her.

'You'd better let me first soothe her irritated senses, dear,' I said, and with one hand, I caressed and played with Fanny's full and voluptuous breasts which I found tense and firm under her sexual excitement, while with the other, I stroked and felt her cunt, a procedure that evidently afforded her considerable relief although, at another time, it doubtless would have provoked shrieks and cries! She had not spent, though she must have been very close to doing it; and I saw that I must watch Alice very closely indeed during the 'turn' she was going to give Fanny for my special delectation, lest the catastrophe I was so desirous of avoiding should occur, for in my mind, I had decided that when Alice had finished tickling Fanny, she should have an opportunity of satisfying her lustful cravings on her, when it would be most desirable that Fanny should be in a condition to show the effect on her of Alice's lascivious exertions.

While feeling Fanny's cunt, I naturally took the opportunity to see if Alice's penetrating finger had met with any difficulty entering and had thus caused Fanny the pain that her shrieks and wriggles had indicated. I found the way in intensely tight, a confirmation of her story and statement that nothing had gone in since the rape was committed on her. Although therefore I could not have the gratification of taking her virginity, I felt positive that I should have a delicious time and that practically, I should be violating her, and I wondered into which of the two delicious cunts now present I would shoot my surging and boiling discharge as it dissolved in Love's sweetest ecstasies!

'Now, Alice, I think she is ready for you!' I said when I had stroked and felt Fanny to my complete satisfaction.

'No, no, Miss Alice!' shrieked Fanny in frantic terror, 'for God's sake, don't tickle me again!'

Disregarding her cries, Alice, who had with difficulty restrained her impatience, quickly again applied the feather to Fanny's cunt, and a wonderful spectacle followed; Fanny's shrieks, cries, entreaties, filled the room while she wiggled and squirmed and twisted herself about in the most bewitchingly provocative manner, while Alice, with parted lips and eyes that simply glistened with lust, remorselessly tickled her maid's cunt with every refinement of cruelty, every fresh shriek and convulsion bringing a delightful look on her tell-tale face. Motionless, I watched the pair, till I noticed Fanny's breasts stiffen and become tense. Immediately I covered her cunt with my hand, saying to Alice: 'Stop, dear, she's had as much as she can stand!' Then reluctantly she desisted from her absorbing occupation and rose, her naked body quivering with aroused but unsatisfied lust.

Now was the time for me to try and effect what I had in mind, viz, the introduction of both girls to Tribadism! 'Let us move Fanny to the large couch and fasten her down before she recovers herself,' I hastily whispered to Alice. Quickly we set her loose, between us we carried her, half-fainting, to the large settee couch where we lay her on her back and made fast her wrists to the two top corners and her ankles to the two lower ones. We now had only to set the machinery going and she would lie in the position I desired, namely spread-eagled!

Alice, now clutched me excitedly and whispered hurriedly: 'Jack, do me before she comes to herself and before she can see us! I'm just mad for it!' And indeed with her flushed cheeks, humid eyes, and heaving breasts this was very evident!

But although I also was bursting with lust and eager to fuck either Alice or her maid, it would not have suited my programme to do so! I wanted Alice to fuck Fanny! I wanted the first spending of both girls to be mutually provoked by the friction of their excited cunts one against the other! This was why I stopped Alice from tickling her maid into spending, and it was for this reason that I had extended Fanny on her back in such a position that her cunt should be at Alice's disposal!

'Hold on, darling, for a bit!' I whispered back, 'you'll soon see why! I want it as badly as you do, my sweet, but am fighting against it till the proper time comes! Run away now, and take off your hat, for it will now be only in the way,' and I smiled significantly as I kissed her.

Alice promptly obeyed. I then seated myself on the couch by the side of Fanny, who was still lying with eyes closed, but breathing almost normally, and bending over her, I closely inspected her cunt to ascertain whether she had or had not spent under the terrific tickling it had just received! I could find no traces whatever, but to make sure I gently drew the lips apart and peered into the sweet coral cleft, but again saw no traces. The touch of my fingers on her cunt however had roused Fanny from her semi-stupor and she dreamily opened her eyes, murmuring: 'Oh, Sir, don't!' as she recognized that I was her assailant, then she looked hurriedly round as in search of Alice.

'Your mistress will be here immediately,' I said with a smile, 'she has only gone away to take off her hat!' The look of terror returned to her eyes, and she exclaimed: 'Oh, Mr Jack, do let me go, she'll kill me!'

'Oh, no!' I replied as I laughed at her agitation, 'oh, no, Fanny, on the contrary she's now going to do to you the sweetest, nicest and kindest thing one girl can do to another! Here she comes!'

I rose as Alice came up full of pleasurable excitement as to what was now going to happen, and slipped my arm lovingly round her waist. She looked eagerly at her now trembling maid, then whispered: 'Is she ready for us again, Jack?'

'Yes, dear!' I answered softly. 'While you were away taking off your hat, I thought it as well to see in what condition her cunt was after its tickling! I find it very much irritated and badly in want of Nature's soothing essence! You, darling, are also much in the same state, your cunt also wants soothing! So I want you girls to soothe each other! Get onto Fanny, dear, take her in your arms; arrange yourself on her so that your cunt lies on hers! and then gently rub yours against hers! and soon both of you will be tasting the sweetest ecstasy!! In other words, fuck Fanny, dear.'

Alice looked at me in wonderous admiration! As she began to comprehend my suggestion, her face broke into delightful smiles; and when I stooped to kiss her she exclaimed rapturously: 'Oh, Jack! how sweet! . . . how delicious!' as she gazed eagerly at Fanny. But the latter seemed horrified at the idea of being submitted thus to her mistress's lustful passion and embraces, and attempted to escape, crying in her dismay: 'No, no, Sir!—oh, no, Miss!—I don't want it, please!. . .'

'But I do, Fanny,' cried Alice with sparkling eyes as she gently but firmly pushed her struggling maid onto her back and held her down forcibly, till I had pulled all four straps tight, so that Fanny lay flat with her arms and legs wide apart in Maltese-Cross fashion, a simply entrancing spectacle! Then slipping my hands under her buttocks, I raised her middle till Alice was able to push a hard cushion under her bottom, the effect of which was to make her cunt stand out prominently; then turning to Alice, who had assisted in these preparations with the keenest interest but evident impatience, I said: 'Now dear, there she is! Set to work and violate your maid!'

In a flash Alice was on the couch and on her knees between Fanny's widely parted legs—excitedly she threw herself on her maid, passed her arms round her and hugged her closely, as she showered kisses on Fanny's still protesting mouth till the girl had to stop for breath. With a few rapid movements she arranged herself on her maid so that the two luscious pairs of breasts were pressing against each other, their stomachs in close contact, and their cunts touching!

'One moment, Alice!' I exclaimed, just as she was beginning to agitate herself on Fanny, 'Let me see that you are properly placed before you start!'

Leaning over her bottom, I gently parted her thighs, till between them I saw the cunts of the mistress and the maid resting on each other, slit to slit, clitoris to clitoris, half hidden by the mass of their closely interwoven hairs, the sweetest of sights! Then, after restoring her thighs to their original position closely pressed against each other, I gently thrust my right hand between the girl's navels, and worked it along amidst their bellies till it lay between their cunts! 'Press down a bit, Alice!' I said, patting her bottom with my disengaged hand; promptly she complied with two or three vigorous down-thrusts which forced my palm hard against Fanny's cunt while her own pressed deliciously against the back of my hand. The sensation of thus feeling at the same time these two full fat fleshy warm and throbbing cunts between which my hand lay in sandwich fashion was something exquisite; and it was with the greatest reluctance that I removed it from the sweetest position it is ever likely to be in, but Alice's restless and involuntary movements proclaimed that she was fast yielding to her feverish impatience to fuck Fanny and to taste the rapture of spending on the cunt of her maid the emission provoked by its sweet contact and friction against her own excited organ!

She still held Fanny closely clasped against her and with head slightly thrown back, she kept her eyes fixed on her maid's terrified averted face with a gloating hungry look, murmuring softly: 'Fanny, you shall now . . . love me!' Both the girls were quivering, Alice from overwhelming and unsatisfied lust, Fanny from shame and horrible apprehension!

Caressing Alice's bottom encouragingly, I whispered: 'Go ahead, dear!' In a trice her lips were pressed to Fanny's flushed cheeks on which she rained hot kisses as she slowly began to agitate her cunt against her maid's with voluptuous movements of her beautiful bottom. 'Oh! Miss . . .' gasped Fanny her eyes betraying the sexual emotion that she felt beginning to overpower her, her colour coming and going! Quicker and more agitated became Alice's movements; soon she was furiously rubbing her cunt against Fanny's with strenuous down-thrusting strokes of her bottom, continuing her fierce kisses on her maid's cheeks as the latter lay helpless with half-closed eyes, tightly clasped in her mistress's arms! Then a hurricane of sexual rage seemed to seize Alice! Her bottom wildly oscillated and gyrated with confused jerks, thrusts, and shoves as she frenziedly pressed her cunt against Fanny's with a rapid jogging motion: suddenly Alice seemed to stiffen and become almost rigid, her arms gripped Fanny more tightly than ever; then her head fell forward on Fanny's shoulder as an indescribable spasm thrilled through her, followed by convulsive vibrations and tremors! Almost simultaneously Fanny's half-closed eyes turned upwards till the whites were showing, her lips parted, she gasped brokenly: 'Oh! . . . Miss . . . Alice! . . . Ah . . . h!' then thrilled convulsively while quiver after quiver shot through her! The blissful crisis had arrived! Mistress and maid were deliriously spending

cunt against cunt, Alice in rapturous ecstasy at having
so deliciously satisfied her sexual desires by means of
her maid's cunt, while forcing the latter to spend in
spite of herself, while Fanny was quivering ecstatically
under heavenly sensations hitherto unknown to her
and now communicated to her wondering senses by
her mistress whom she still felt lying on her and in
whose arms she was still clasped!

My Conversion

**Translated from the French by
Howard Nelson**

Back in the Babylon which has the most corruption of any city in the world simply because it has the most people, I wore myself out paying calls on every coquette and scoundrel in Paris. For more than two weeks nothing eventful happened. I was bored to tears. I gambled and lost. I saw that my sustenance would be gone if I continued, and so I considered flight to avoid the temptation of the tables. It was a momentous decision which I carefully weighed.

Already the sun was gilding the crops and the Graces were retreating to the copses. And all the women were flying to the countryside. Their example decided me and I followed them. You can be sure that like a busy bee I sucked only the juiciest blossoms. Nevertheless, it was tedious.

You know as well as I those enchanted palaces that line the shores of the peaceful Seine. I went there and found nothing.

Finally, I went to the Marne where rise walls built by our forefathers. Their imposing aspect seems to proclaim that kings reside there. But no. It is merely the abode of the brides of Our Saviour, the convent of ***, whose abbess is the aunt of one of my acquaintances. She has been told that I am likeable and I am welcomed with open arms. You have no idea of the excitement I cause when I arrive. The pretty little nun coquettishly adjusts her wimple when she sees me. All rush to the visiting room.

When Madame Abbess appears, all vanish out of

respect. What a voluptuous figure she has. I could almost eat her.

She has just reached her fifth lustrum. To the flower of youthfulness is joined the blossom of perfect health. A glittering face with eyes blacker than jet, a rose-bordered mouth, and teeth of ivory that she permits me to admire. There is something of the flirt about her which her garb cannot conceal.

When she notes the lust in my eyes, she says to me teasingly: 'Are you another Abelard?'

I don't know what to say. But I know that I am going to fuck my Abbess or know the reason why. The compliments we exchange are prettily turned on her part and gallant on mine. Soon we are chatting as if we had known each other for years. My God! Now I have an erection that is killing me. It is the result of gazing too intently at those seductive breasts.

I shall not speak of the parties that were given in my honour or the recitals. There could be heard my sonorous male voice blending with the titters of the timid novices. A satyr is loose among captive nymphs, in effect. In vain do they try to flee, but there is something about me that stops their steps. As they totter, the squeals they emit are not those of fear.

What a wonderful thing to find yourself in a seraglio of twenty little nuns who vie with one another in loveliness. Their eyes reveal a tender languor. Several of the innocents have twitches they have never before experienced. How sweet they look. Let's fuck. Let's fuck. Oh, my prick, show what you are capable of. Hail Venus! Hail Priapus!

Contemplating such matters, I toss about in my bed. I am unable to sleep because of my excitement.

The next day, Madame the Abbess is slightly indisposed and keeps to her bed. I receive permission to pay my respects in her apartment.

What has come over me? She is as lovely as an angel. I forget why I have come. She extends her hand to me as she asks about my health. With passion I kiss that hand. She gives a sigh. Another sigh is my response. We are alone. Her half-closed eyes, her fluttering eyelashes, the distension of her stomach, and the palpitation of an alabaster bosom still covered by an inopportune veil embolden me. 'Julia! Julia!' Such are the first sparks of our fires. I kneel at the side of the bed with my burning lips on the hand that I did not relinquish. She makes no attempt to snatch it away. Heavens! She has fainted. She is dying. I summon her servants with screams of terror. Salts, waters, scents!

'That's one of Madame's dizzy spells,' cries one of the maids.

But it is not her final attack. After a quarter of an hour, she returns to her senses, pale as a sheet. Her pallor, however, is that of a woman in love. Several tears have dampened her beseeching eyes. Finally, we are by ourselves again.

'I apologize for these attacks which nearly kill me. The doctors cannot seem to diagnose them.'

I note the colour returning to her cheeks. Her pulse becomes normal. My heart is pounding as I approach her. Several disarranged pillows offer me a pretext. As I advance my hand to straighten them and hold her up—oh wonder of wonders!—her opulent bosom is offered to my view. The sight intoxicates me. I press my amorous mouth against her amorous mouth. My tongue gives her quivers of voluptuousness. Gradually, I make my way to the sanctuary. A finger penetrates it. It gives a twitch, one which excites her still more. What ineffable bliss!

'Sweet Jesus!' she moans. 'I can't stand this wonderful feeling. I think I am expiring.'

The sensations are too much, too new. Unable to withstand the shock, I sink back in a faint. She is worried to such an extent that she rings for her maid. When I come to, I find myself in their arms. Their efforts to revive me are so successful that the petite maid, on seeing the condition I am in, deems it wise to retire. The Abbess and I reiterate a thousand times our vows to love each other eternally, and after each oath, we seal it with the appropriate ceremony.

I am nourished with the strongest broths and foods. I spend the day as I did the morning, and the night is just as joyful. The following days, diversions without number are prepared for me—hunting, fishing and games. Such thoughtfulness strengthens my ties to the Abbess even more firmly. She is lascivious without being coarse. She takes my advice and my lessons inflame her. Her lovely svelte and flexible body and her shapely legs enlace me, melt into my body. Only in my arms does she enjoy repose.

I would have been true to her, but the flesh is weak. Young hearts are pining for me, and should I let them wither and fade away? No, I am too compassionate.

I establish a schedule—my nights are with the Abbess and my days are occupied otherwise. The dormitories and cells are all open to me, and I take advantage of it. The first one I fuck is discreet.

Discreet? You must be joking.

I am not. It is with the maid who restored me. And that's the truth. She was in charge of my meals. One day, I was so excited by the chase that I return late.

She is not expecting me. I enter her cell. Guess what meets my eyes.

She is sprawled out in a big armchair with her robe lifted up to her navel and her legs spread wide apart. With a great deal of enthusiasm she is manipulating—a dildo!

I shut the door quickly. Precipitately, she drops her petticoat and leaves the spear in the wound. With a deep blush, she stands up and starts to walk away with her thighs squeezed closely together. The devil inspires me. Taking her under the arms, I free Priapus who soon finds refuge deep in the centre of the comfortable chamber. She makes a feeble protest.

'My dear, I caught you in the act. And I am going to finish what you started. Don't worry. I won't betray you.'

I lay her on the couch, where I perform the sweet task twice.

'God bless you,' she sighs when it is over.

One day, the Abbess beckoned me and led me to a cell. Putting her finger to her lips, she pointed to a peephole and motioned me to have a look through it. I did as I was bid and saw Sister Stephanie in the adjoining cubicle.

Dear Sister Stephanie—such a romantic name. Young, rosy cheeked and ash blonde, she reminded me of a bouquet of flowers with her gentle charming voice and her veiled look which seemed to conceal so many tender secrets.

And the cell. It was a weird world, a bizarre enclosure whose walls were not limed with white but with blue, a sky blue that was almost ethereal. The ceiling, too, was painted with the same azure while

118

the floor was of carefully waxed white planks. The bed looked comfortable.

What was out of place in the nun's cell was a Christ nailed to an oversized cross bracketed to the wall, but the figure was not that of the emaciated Saviour that is so familiar. He was a robust male with powerful pectoral muscles. Moreover, the body was made of a material with an astonishing resemblance to human flesh. I saw Stephanie touch it and her finger sank in.

As for the face of the Christ, the expression was one of ecstasy, a profane rapture that had absolutely nothing to do with religious exaltation. It was a hand-some face, masculine and virile. The nostrils and lips were sensual, and there was a glitter in the eyes.

The door opened and in stepped Angela, one of the more delicious of the novices, who was warmly welcomed with a kiss.

'What lovely hair you have,' Stephanie remarked.

'And how about yours, Sister Stephanie?'

'I am rather vain about it.'

'But I thought when you took your vows, you had to have your head shaved.'

'Yes, you do. But if you get on the good side of the Mother Superior, she gives you permission to let it grow and fix it any way you like. It goes without saying that you can't let it show. Certain nuns would understand these special marks of favour.'

'Show me your hair,' Angela demanded.

Without any hesitation, the woman removed her wimple, and a cascade of tresses tumbled down over her shoulders. Silky curls, elegant waves fell on the white starched collar that formed a part of her costume.

After a gasp of unfeigned admiration, Angela asked permission to brush it.

The girl sat down facing the sister and began to brush the hair with measured strokes. Suddenly, Stephanie kissed Angela's lips with her moist mouth. At first, the girl shrank back but then surrendered her lips and tongue. In a trice her body was embraced. I could see that her sex was being ignited. The sensation must have become even more unbearable when Stephanie caressed the yearning breasts through the blouse. Then, baring them, she took the nipples in her mouth and sucked them slowly and avidly.

'I think I have wet myself,' Angela murmured.

Finally, Sister Stephanie disrobed, exhibiting her nude body with arrogance and hauteur. She possessed opulent round breasts, a thick fleece, smooth thighs, and delicious buttocks.

With deft nimble hands, she quickly divested the girl of her clothing, pushed her back on the bed and began to fondle her ardently.

I could see that Angela had lost touch with reality and I surmised that this was the first time she was experiencing true voluptuousness. Her twitches soon became violent convulsions.

She sank back in a faint from the force of the sensations. But she recovered under the tingling caresses that the sister was bestowing between her open thighs with her agile darting tongue. Then I heard the enamoured sighs, the squeals of joy, and the prolonged moans of pleasure which announced the arrival of the supreme sensation.

They fell back in exhaustion, but I kept my eye glued to the aperture. After a few moments, Stephanie rose and left the bed. I followed her with my eyes as she went to the Christ, pressed herself to it, embraced his muscular thighs, and licked his face. Now she stepped back and began undoing the loin cloth. When it dropped down to the floor, I observed to my astonishment that crucifixion did not necessarily cause loss of virility. And what virility! It was a long member which swayed and vibrated, a foully atrractive object the like of which I had never seen. Although it was monstrous, I found it strangely attractive, and I could recognize that this organ nestled between hairy bloated sacks could promise a woman certain raptures.

Stunned with amazement, I watched Sister Stephanie slowly impale herself on the colossus. As she let herself slowly down it, she shuddered and gave little groans. Now she slowly jabbed herself with it in a regular cadence. The cheeks of her buttocks were tightly closed to augment the sensation.

Now the nun began an almost motionless dance which ended with a loud shout followed by a long obscene rattle.

Let's pass over in silence several rather ordinary incidents. I fucked Sister Lapine, Sister Magdelon, Mother Bonaventure, etc. The dormitory, the garden, the dispensary and the chapel are all the theatres of my exploits. But let's discuss the novices.

They are five, and among them, Sisters Agatha, Rose and Agnes stand out. They are the most adorable creatures imaginable. The first two are inseparable and play with each other for lack of anything better to do. Agnes is in love with me, but she hides her feelings and weeps to herself. One day, I find the means to share her room with her.

'What's wrong with you, Agnes?' I demand of her.

'I really don't know.'

'For the last week, something has come over you. You are completely different. You used to laugh and be so much fun, but now you just look out into space and sigh. Tell me what's wrong. Or don't you trust me, who loves you so much?'

She flushes. 'You do love me? If only that were so.'

'Have I offended you?' I ask, taking her hand.

'Please leave me. I don't feel well.'

She rises.

'I see that you are afraid of me. Perhaps I am hateful to you. I think it is about time for me to leave.'

'You're not going?' she cries.

Poor child. She's mine. No further effort is needed. I shall soon have her.

The head of the novices provides me with a good opportunity a few days later. You will recall that she is a good friend. The choir is supposed to sing a motet, but the music-master does not come, and so she confides Agnes to me for the rehearsal.

As soon as the good sister closes the door on us, I resume my attack: 'Lovely Agnes, are you always so cruel?'

She lowers her eyes.

'How unhappy I am. Only God knows how much.'

She raises her hands to heaven.

'Agnes, you have made tears come to my eyes.'

'What do you think about me. I have been crying my heart out.'

Her tears fall fast and heavy.

'Let us console each other. If we don't, I shall die.'

'No,' she sobs. 'You cannot die. It is I who shall have to.'

I take her and put her on my knee with her head against my face.

'Agnes, it is only you whom I love. Tell me that you love me, too.'

'You wicked man, how can you have any doubt about that?'

Her mouth grazes my lips. The child does not recognize the significance of the outbursts of her heart. Her hour is come. I cover her with kisses. I transfer into her heart the fire that is devouring me. I make her drunk with caresses and kisses. When I remove the last of the veils, I am stunned by the treasures that are revealed. Modesty no longer holds me back. She no longer knows what she is doing. Like a flash of lightning, I strip her bare. The scream that Agnes lets escape is the signal of my victory.

You are probably thinking, fool that you are, that she makes a painful face and puts on airs and that she is despising me as her rapist. On the contrary, she thanks me from the bottom of her heart, the poor child. It is true that I merit the praise, for the fortress is damnably difficult to take.

Afterwards we begin work on her part in the motet. When the Mother Superior returns, Agnes is singing with the voice of an angel. As for myself, I am scorched and scalded. But twelve hours of repose heal my scars.

What a way to spend your time.

What do you mean, you fault-finder?

I'm scolding you because you are wasting your time without getting any money.

Oh, I forgot to tell you that the Abbess was the soul of generosity. No woman has ever been so bountiful. Now that your fears are calmed, let me continue with the account of my exploits.

Sisters Agatha and Rose are deserving of my homage. The elder cannot be more than eighteen. The former, possessed of an irrepressible spirit, has the devil in her flesh. Rose is more thoughtful but gay at the same time. These two children are united by a mutual understanding. The Abbess, whose jewels they are, told me in confidence that more than once she allowed them in her bed to appease their desires. The excesses they gave themselves up to! When I give them dancing instruction, we do all sorts of silly things.

'Sisters,' I say one day, 'would you be good enough to show me the games you play with each other.'

'What games?' demands Agatha as Rose blushes.

'If I knew, I wouldn't be asking you.'

'Well, Rose, I think he means hide-and-seek.' She begins to giggle.

'There's nothing hidden,' I tell them sternly. 'I saw everything.

'What?' asks Rose in consternation. 'You saw? Agatha, we are lost.'

Both begin to weep.

'Dry your tears,' I order them. 'I promise I won't say a word.'

That reassures them somewhat. Besides, what they have done is considered in a convent only a little sin.

'But how were you able to spy on us?' Agatha timidly asks me.

'I really didn't see you. A little genie told me what you were doing.'

'A genie?' she exclaims.

'A genie? echoes Rose.

'Yes, a genie who comes to me every day. (I can barely stifle my roars of laughter.) I'll introduce you to him on the condition that you teach me your game and that you listen to what he has to say.'

'What? Does he speak, and how?'

'We talk to each other in sign language. I'll explain later.'

'Let's see.'

'Yes, let's see,' chimes in Rose.

'Easy,' I warn them. 'Wait until I summon him. In the meantime, perhaps you would like to show me your game. . . .'

(I had my reasons, but never has my jinni been so recalcitrant. I did my best to spur him to action, but nothing occurred. Finally, the imp arrived. Here is what happened. I produce the Monsignor, which makes Agatha's eye pop. She springs towards it.)

'Oh, Rose, I have it in my hand. Look at how beautifully it is fashioned. But it doesn't have any nose!'

'Help me to hold it lest it fly away.'

Rose clutches it.

'How quickly it came.' She tries to unhinge it.

'Young ladies, just a moment. Don't you see that it is just a little snail. It's in its shell.'

'That's so,' Rose says. 'Look at it in its cushion.'

'I've never seen a snail like this one,' Agatha comments.

'It's probably from China.'

'Where are its feelers?'

I am dying of fear lest I should be emancipated in their tender hands.

'I think he wishes to speak,' I tell them.

125

'We would like to hear him,' they reply.

'I have to warn you that if you get him angry, he will go away and never return. Now, mum's the word.'

I grasp Agatha and throw her on the bed. She is a brave little thing, not uttering a word. In a moment, I have her skirt up to her waist. Wild with curiosity, Rose flutters around.

'Agatha, is he speaking?'

'Oh, yes. I have never heard such eloquence. I don't think I can stand it any more.'

'What is he saying?'

It goes without saying that she has other things to do than reply. The little she-devil wiggles so divinely that I am about to begin all over again, when Rose, unable to contain herself any longer, grabs me. The overheated perspiring genie emerges from the carnage and begins to work on Agatha's companion. Although she is not as vivacious, she is almost mad with voluptuousness. But she has that rare quality I have always appreciated in a woman—the door of the sanctuary closes after the sacrifice without leaving me time to go limp. By now, neither of them is plying me with questions. They are in a state of utter ecstasy. As for myself, I take keen enjoyment in their confusion. We no longer speak of the game. They realize that they have been fooled, but they hold me no grudge.

I am at the peak of bliss, although somewhat fatigued. Every time I consider giving up the game, the devil comes out of his hiding-place and spurs me to new efforts.

Life becomes heaven and hell. You remember that three goddesses fought for one apple. Well, imagine what it is like when twenty little eager nuns compete for one man.

My friend, you have no idea of a female republic whose doge is the Abbess. The majority of the girls have been enrolled in the celestial militia against their wills. Although they are the wives of an ethereal being, they still have corporeal desires. The result is a charnel revolt, a conflict between the senses and reason, between the Creator and the creature. All that stimulates the passions, irritates desires and inflames imagination. That is why the girls get spasms and nervous attacks. They can't be praying all the time.

The normal object of their adoration is the confessor. If there are two, they share the fold, each hating the other cordially. If there is only one, the lambs fight among themselves for his favours.

'What! Over an old monk?'

'Yes. Over an old monk. They would do anything for him, for at least he is of flesh rather than wood or metal.'

Consequently, in these abodes of peace and innocence, one enjoys all the comforts of hell.

If only you knew the ruses the girls employ to sneak their lovers over the walls. I could tell you of the horrors of the despotism the vicious old women wield over their charges. There take place orgies worthy of being described by Aretino. When they are married, they have been initiated into every vice imaginable.

The murmurs of discontent are becoming louder. The governing body holds a session. Fault is found with the Abbess who demands that her tastes and pleasures be respected. The reverend mothers are all ears as they eavesdrop. The little innocents are trembling with fear. The way they all look at me leads me to believe that I'll be the scapegoat. For fear of losing me, the Abbess stoutly defends me. The complaints are brought to the attention of the Bishop and thick-witted priest, who announces that he is coming in person to restore order in a house into which Belial has insinuated himself. I am ready to face him, but my dear Abbess persuades me that if I stay, she will be ruined. Loaded with sugar and gold, I make my departure. There is scarcely a dry eye when I leave.

The House of Borgia

Cesare stretched himself at ease on the red plush couch which had been put at his disposal. Around him, his principal officers shared with their leader the privilege of being the guest of the Chief Councillor of the city. Outside, the cannon was quiet, the citadel comfortably besieged. Full-scale assault operations could wait until tomorrow. The army needed rest and a little entertainment.

Throughout the city the brothels were doing fine, wine-flushed business. And any woman who showed herself willing was feeling the full pent-up strength following days of abstinence on the part of the visitors between her thighs. But, as usual, Cesare had forbidden violence. Any man reported stealing a citizen's unwilling wife or raping a reluctant maiden would be made an example of for all the town to see.

Within the mansion of the Chief Councillor, gypsy music was playing. A band of well-dressed nomads were strumming their guitars and tambourines. There was controlled passion in the music and in the dark, gypsy faces. There was ill-controlled passion, too, in the loins of Cesare's officers. This man, their host, had promised them, later, the full benefits of the high-class brothel which was virtually his harem. They were anxious to relieve this ache of longing in their lower regions.

Cesare toyed with his glass, sipping the rich, sweet wine with which his host had bolstered a magnificent meal. He was thinking of Lucrezia, wishing she were here, now, so that they could retire to a quiet nook and enjoy each other with the furious abandon of the days before he had left for the French Court.

'How do you like my gypsy orchestra?' his host asked, leaning across from his neighbouring couch.

'Excellent, excellent, but they look a little domesticated.'

'You mean they are well dressed, well fed? But of course. They have become quite famous these last few months. Everybody is paying big prices to have them play and dance. Their days of dirt and rags are over.'

He swallowed a glass of wine in one long draught.

'But if you talk of domestication, wait until you see Maria. Domestication! I'd like to see the man who could domesticate her. Violence, passion, sensuality! They ripple in her limbs when she dances, they reach to you from her breasts, they writhe in her buttocks. And yet she's not for sale. Oh, they've tried to rape her—many a man in torment. But she carries a stiletto and knows how to use it, they say. She's a proud one. I have to rush to my mistress in excitement after she's danced, and then I try to imagine she's the divine Maria who won't be bought.'

Cesare listened, idly swishing the wine in his refilled glass and letting the music flow in him. The old dotard, he was thinking; the thought that he couldn't have her would make him pay grovelling homage to the ugliest old whore.

'Well, when does this proud creature deign to appear?' he asked.

'Immediately if you so wish it.'

The host clapped his hands and gave orders to a servant, who disappeared, gliding over the rich carpets which covered the tiled floor, into the other rooms which led off from a portico at the far end of the main dining hall.

After a few minutes, he reappeared, gave a few whispered instructions to the leader of the gypsy ochestra and withdrew.

The music changed suddenly to a wild, passionate flamenco in true Spanish style, the notes hurtling and gyrating one after the other in a loud, fiery torrent. There was a sudden strumming of chords and then a lowering of tempo and pitch. The guest officers glanced up from their conversation and wine. There was a foreboding in the music which immediately attracted all attention. While they stared, not knowing quite what to expect, but certain that something was going to happen, a figure danced slowly in from the shadows of the portico, a shadowy movement at first, growing into a flame of red and black, becoming a beautiful girl who swayed sensually in before the gypsy band which accompanied her.

There was an instant tension in the assembly. Men who had been engaged in, at least, the semblance of war for more than a week or two, flushed over with the tightening of desire. Cesare put down the glass with which he had been describing circles in the air.

'You hardly exaggerated,' he said quietly and in some surprise.

'Almost worth a stiletto in the ribs if one could be certain of achieving one's fill before the death blow, eh?' chuckled his host.

Cesare Borgia didn't reply. His thoughts were away on the hips that revolved gently, the breasts that were taut from her upstretched, slender brown arms. Her face seemed to spark and blaze with pride and a controlled sensuality; her dark hair swept back, dropping, long onto her shoulders; broad brow over dark, almond eyes, a straight nose which flared lightly at the nostrils, long, full lips which opened often in intense concentration as she danced, a good, clear chin which was round and smooth under her mouth; and then the neck, long and unexpectedly well-developed as she came forward into the light, full and with the slight ridge of a vein; below the black lace frill of the tight-bodiced red dress she wore, the breasts which forced out the yielding stuff in strong, taut lines, the slim waist which moved and writhed inside the dress, the skirt tight over her hips, enclosing her buttocks in a tight embrace and then flaring out loosely around her thighs to permit her freedom of movement.

'Superb, superb,' Cesare murmured aloud and his host smiled with a pleasure that conflicted with his mask of almost miserable longing.

The music gathered in crescendo and the girl made a full, twirling tour of the room, skimming the tables of the spectators with her flying skirt. She seemed to see nobody. At times her face was serene and ethereal, at others working with passion as if she were in the throes of sexual intercourse. The men seemed to come to life, out of the still, electric petrification her arrival had induced. They slithered forward on their couches the better to see. There were odd comments of coarse appreciation uttered without a withdrawal of the eyes watching her every movement, every crease and tension of every part of her body under the flaming silk dress.

The Duke of Valentinois watched with the others. He felt his heart pounding and that empty sucking in his stomach. She was as beautiful as Lucrezia, this

Maria, the gypsy; as beautiful at the other end of the scale, each of them perfection of their own kind.

His eyes ran over her avidly. As she swayed toward his end of the room, slim arms flowering in the light of the candles around the walls, he watched her breasts, full and alive under the slender covering. They bulged and moved in unison with her movement. The points of her nipples jutted, large and voluptuous from the summits of the warm mounds of flesh behind them. He let his glance fall, taking in the slim waist, so slim that it moved all by itself inside the dress as if it wanted no part of these protecting clothes. And then the tight containment of those hips, the rounded belly, which could be cupped with a hand, the protrusion of hipbones, well-fleshed and bulging against the silk, the lines of the strong, sexual thighs and then the slim, lightly-muscled calves that twirled below the whirl of the skirts.

'Beautiful, beautiful,' Cesare whispered.

His host leaned toward him, hotly.

'You must forgive me,' he muttered. 'I can't bear to stay. It is a mistake for me to be here at all and I must take my leave in a few moments. If there is anything you or your officers require of me, you have only to ask my servants. They will show you to your quarters and to the source of your future enjoyment.'

His breath had come with difficulty and when Cesare looked at him he saw that his face was almost crimson and his eyes drawn in anguish.

'My poor Chief Councillor,' he whispered sympathetically, 'I understand your predicament. To have such a delight within your house and be unable to sip of the ecstasy she promises is hard indeed. But I crave one boon before you leave—that I may be permitted to try my gallantry with the lady.'

There was a note of envy in the Chief Councillor's tone as he gazed into Cesare's handsome, commanding face.

'By all means,' he said, 'and I wish you success. Perhaps a conquest would soften her heart toward others who would give their souls to share her bed. I will see that she joins you alone after the entertainment and that you are not disturbed.'

With that the Chief Councillor rose, not waiting even to hear his guest's thanks, and slipped from the banquet hall as if he were afraid he would in some way disgrace himself if he delayed his exit a single second.

Grinning to himself, Cesare turned back to the spectacle. The music was throbbing, drugging the room with its heavy insistence. The girl had her back to him, arms high above her head, hips swaying, heels tapping on the marble floor. The outlines of her buttocks pressed and relaxed in firm ovals against the seat of the dress. Each seemed to move of its own accord, rounded and naked, inviting lustful attack. She whirled and flitted forward with flying, little steps, toward Cesare's table. Her eyes seemed to catch his for an instant. He held them and they bored back at him until slowly he dropped his gaze and stared meaningfully at the triangular crease of her dress between her thighs. When he glanced up again, her eyes were still on him, but flicked away immediately, her head bowing to the ground in concentration.

A hot glow consumed Cesare, slowly, from his genitals. He had no thought of failure. The meeting of their eyes had established the beginning. He would, as always, win.

For a moment, he took his eyes from the scene to witness its effect. His officers were hypnotized. Some faces were scarlet, others white with desire: a band of civilized men, suddenly naked and primitive in the face of elemental sexual passion. The difference between most of them and himself, Cesare knew, was the difference between himself and the Chief Councillor: that he would not give his soul to possess this woman. It was, also, this very aloof quality which communicated itself even in moments of intimacy, which gave him his extraordinary power of attracting and, if desired, maintaining the interest of the most difficult and independent of women. Cesare had learned from his sister, Lucrezia, the intricacies of intrigue and attitude that women were capable of; he had, perhaps, been fortunate in learning from her the necessity of keeping himself beyond the snares which they set, of keeping himself whole in mind and emotions, of being always the master.

Now, catching again the eyes of the beautiful gypsy girl as she danced toward him, letting his eyes rove insolently over her breasts as if he were stroking them with his eyelashes, he felt certain that she was his. He could hardly wait to hold those buttocks naked in his hands and drive his strength and mastery between her naked thighs into the conquered lips that waited softly to receive him.

It was very warm in the banquet hall—as if all those who had left had jettisoned their heat before departure. Not all the candles still glowed smoothly into the gloom, only a few at odd points around the walls cast deep and slightly moving shadows. There were two red candles flickering on the table and they threw a warm, flattering light on the faces of Cesare and the gypsy girl.

'A little wine,' Cesare was saying, as he filled her glass again.

She took her long-stemmed glass and sipped, looking at him over its rim. Her eyes were warm, and so friendly that they would have turned over the Chief Councillor's heart had he been there.

'They say that you will soon be lord of all Romagna—perhaps of all Italy,' she said softly.

'Gossip,' Cesare said. 'But it may be true.' He smiled. 'My chances would be greater had I your power of reducing men to willing slavery.'

'Gossip,' she retorted, 'if we speak of men. I can think of many I would not put in that category.'

'Our poor Chief Councillor is slowly dying of suffocation—suffocation of his desires.'

'He is like a cow,' she said. 'He chews his food and watches me with great, gawking eyes. When he desired me he had to send a servant to try to procure me so afraid was he that I might spit in his face.'

Cesare took a long gulp of wine.

'Are all as unlucky as he?'

'Did he not tell you I'm not to be bought?'

'I'm not talking of buying.'

She raised an eyebrow at him over her glass and smiled. She gave no answer and Cesare put his hand on hers on the table, gently but firmly.

'You remind me of my sister Lucrezia,' he said.

'But isn't she blonde?'

'I mean that you are perfect in your particular beauty as she is in hers. I am told, too, that she is perfect in bed. As for that, I would never be able to compare you.'

He watched her closely. But she didn't take his words amiss. Clearly he was not in the same class as the Chief Councillor, nor had she removed her hand from his.

'What happens when you want to give—and not be bought?' he asked.

'These are very personal questions—I had heard you were very direct,' she said, still smiling.

'It's the only way to know people,' he replied. 'Hedging and social protocol are all very well in their place.'

'Yes,' she said and she turned her hand in his and entwined their fingers gently. 'I have given very rarely,' she went on. 'I only give when I'm moved, otherwise it's not worth the pestering which would follow from all those who assume that because a woman gives she is free to all.'

She had leaned forward slightly and Cesare could see deep down between the swellings of her breasts. The skin was a tawny flame-colour and as smooth looking as parchment. He let his eyes run from her breasts up over her shoulders and that strong, voluptuous neck. When his eyes reached hers she was looking at him without the smile. It had been replaced by a look he recognized—Lucrezia's look of desire. In those few seconds he thought with amazement that she must always have looked like this. That even in rags, running the streets of the slum quarters in her youth before she joined the gypsy band, she looked this same lovely, haughty, sensual woman who might, at that time, have given herself to anyone who was prepared to make her rich, to give her the life of a lady. He wondered that no rich merchant, straying on his horse through the poor quarter, had caught a glimpse of her—probably with half a breast naked through her rags and tatters, or a side view of a straining buttock. She could, by now, have been at the court of kings.

'What are you thinking?' she asked softly, the desire still heavy in her eyes. 'Why do you look at me like that?' He looked at the dark shadows below her high, smooth cheekbones, his glance lingered on those full lips which had hardly moved as she spoke.

'I was thinking that you are, perhaps, more beautiful even than Lucrezia,' he said quietly.

'She would not be flattered to hear you say that.'

'She would probably retort by claiming that she was far superior in the boudoir.'

'But even after tonight you would have no way of comparing us—you would never have slept with her.'

Cesare stood up, slowly, not taking his eyes off the girl. Mingled with his unexpectedly easy triumph was a sly amusement at her peasant assumption. He was tempted to tell her, but the moment was not to be spoiled and, in any case, her tongue might wag.

He walked around the table toward her and she stood up with her lips parted, waiting. When he reached her and caught her face in both his hands, her body swept in and wriggled against him. Sparks seemed to fly in his body. God, he thought, it's almost as if she divined and were determined to prove herself the better. The flesh, smoothly, glossily almost, covering the fine bones of her face was hot under his fingers. There was a delicate perfume of roses about her hair. Her lips were moist and gave like a sponge, opening under his. They seemed to swallow his mouth—and then her tongue, smooth as milk was panting into his mouth, exploring it, brushing against his own. Along his whole length he felt the warm slender solidity of her body pressing and moving slightly—the weight of her breasts protruding, the smooth roundness of her thighs brushing and clinging to his, her hips and that excruciating abdominal area which pressed against his confined genitals and slithered against them hotly. He pulled his mouth from hers and she let it go reluctantly. Audible little pantings breathed through her lips, now released, as he moved down her neck, sucking it, biting it, drawing a pattern of little red marks on the velvety skin. He reached her shoulders, the top halves, naked halves, of her breasts, which bulged and wanted to escape and soar forth for him in their entirety. As he bit her breasts gently, her abdomen, that triangular section between her strong thighs, squirmed furiously against the mound of his genitals which she could feel in an erect hump beneath his clothes.

'Let's go through to the private chambers,' he whispered.

'No, now—here!' she said passionately.

He pushed her gently back toward the divan from which he'd watched her dancing earlier in the evening. The Chief Councillor had promised they would be alone—and what did it matter if a servant did tumble onto them? Guilt and fear were for the weak and subordinate.

She fell back onto the couch and he lowered himself down with her. She put her hand on the covered heat of his penis and he felt its trembling, demanding pressure with a wild surge of immediate desire. He began, quickly, to slip off her clothes and she helped him, breathing heavily, looking at him with deep, fire-filled eyes, concentrating on ridding herself of the garments that hid her body from him.

In a matter of seconds she was stretched out on the couch, more naked than in the days of flimsy rags and Cesare's mouth was avidly sucking her large, erect nipples, as his hands flared over her body, exploring its firm, beautiful contours while his penis seemed to throb and hum like a hive of bees.

Her breasts were taut and high in spite of their size. The nipples that he sucked crowned them in a dark, hard summit which seemed to epitomize her desire; the hard bosses yielded and flipped back in rubbering resilience and seemed to reach out to him in pleading desire for assuagement. Below her breasts her hard, narrow waist was the pivot for her writhing hips. No bones showed in her hips, the flesh was full and rounded, the little bulge of her abdomen heaving in and out with its crest of fine, dark hair. Her sensual, well-holding thighs pressed and slithered against each other, opening wide from time to time as Cesare's hands moved over her flesh. Between them, dark rose lips, moist and ready, were crushed with her movement.

Cesare's penis felt wet inside his clothes and the throbbing was unbearable. When, without opening her eyes or stopping the convulsions of her lost body, the girl put her hand again on his penis and began to squeeze and caress it, he stood up quickly and began to tear off his clothes.

She lay there, her breath exploding from between her parted lips, her thighs tight together as if to keep the sensation locked tightly in. She opened her eyes after a few seconds and watched Cesare baring his body. Her eyes were in anguish and her hands, which had moved up to the breasts on which the heat and fury of his lips remained, twitched gently.

Feeling the warm air strike his suddenly naked flesh with a cooling draught, Cesare looked back at the girl's body as he stripped. She was beautiful as a Greek statue and burning with sexual life. He could worship a body like that—except that he didn't worship bodies. He had a sudden irreverent thought of the envy the Chief Councillor would feel when he knew. What that man would give to be here now in his shoes—or rather in his skin.

Nude at last, with his penis soaring ruggedly out and up at an acute angle with his belly, Cesare moved toward the couch. She watched him come, her eyes flowing over his face and from it down over his lightly haired and muscular chest to the slim hips dominated by that great boom of penis with its narrowing, fiery tip. As he reached the divan she reached up and grasped it and icy darts shot through his belly and clashed in his genitals.

He lay down beside her and she stroked and caressed his prick and smothered his lips with hers, flicking her tongue in what seemed an almost involuntary spasm of sensuality.

Cesare pressed her dark head back onto the couch. The rose perfume was all around like an ethereal cushion and her dark hair brushed softly against his face as he sank into her lips and sucked them and her tongue into his mouth. Her flesh was hot and receptive, trembling against his as he slid his hand down over those firm, reaching breasts and the belly with its little indentation and then over the fine hair which was warm and soothing to his fingers, and so between those hot and slightly sweating thighs, right at their topmost point where they merged into the hot arch containing the point of desire.

She gasped as his hand reached the lips of her cunt, gasped into his mouth and was unable to keep her lips against his with the sudden sensation. She dragged her head away and turned it so that her cheek lay along the divan, pressing into it as if she were resisting some torture.

Through the loose, wet flesh, his fingers wandered and into the suddenly tight and opening hole which he found.

'Oh, oh!' she gasped and bit her lips under his passionate, watching eyes as he lay with his cheek against hers. Her hand on his prick redoubled its activity and she began to stroke him gently, moving her fingers lightly on the hot, stiff flesh.

He felt her thighs moving and then opening widely and her crotch rose up slightly toward him, facilitating and demanding the entry of his searching fingers into the moist channel at whose entrance they dawdled. He pressed in, wiping a finger around the elastic rim and plunging on into the depths of the cavern beyond.

'Oh, oh, oh, oh!' Her face on the couch swung back at his and she released his prick and held him tightly with both arms as she kissed him wildly and rubbed her face all over and around his.

Cesare could feel his prick, hot and waiting, pressing up against her hip, the cool, yielding flesh of her hip. He moved in against her, crushing it against that flesh, rubbing his loins against her, moving one of his thighs half over hers.

His finger, now, had penetrated all the way and he could feel the smooth, viscid roof of the cavern. Her thighs alternately clamped his hand in the pressure of a vice and released it, sweeping apart in a wild, passionate gesture. She was panting continuously and punctuating the panting with little moans as he moved his fingertip gently against the roof of the cavern.

Her lovely lips were trembling and her nostrils were slightly flared the way he'd noticed them as she concentrated on her dancing. She had closed her eyes and the long lashes made tremulous shadows on her cheeks. Her long, slim hands ran convulsively over his body, not seeming to be controlled by her at all.

Cesare moved another finger into her vagina and she cringed away and then pushed back on the double prong which filled her. He allowed his fingers to roam all over and through the moist channel of her sex and then slowly withdrew them and searched for the tiny stub of her passion. He found it, hard and erect. It evaded him from time to time as he caressed it, slipping away into the fleshy folds of her lips.

The touch of his fingers on her clitoris had sparked even greater depths of passion reaction from her. She had caught his penis again and squeezed it hard. She ran her fingertips over his balls as far down as she could reach. She brought up her head and bit his neck and lips. She was like a tigress.

Caressing her, tantalizing her, bringing her to a pitch of excitement, with his own thunderous, growing passion as a controlled background, Cesare felt her thigh slipping and digging under his trying to get him to mount her. Her arms pulled his face onto her chest over against her breasts which strained up, digging him with erect, large nipples.

'Now, now,' she murmured. 'Do it now.'

Overcome with a nervous excitement, now that the

moment had come, as if afraid of the power of his own passion, Cesare hesitated, drawing his fingertips up her hard, little clitoris for a few seconds longer until she was groaning with ecstasy.

'Please, please, now, now, now,' she begged, hardly able to utter the words, squeezing blindly on his rod of flesh.

Cesare slithered over onto her. She made a superb, warm cushion for his body. Her thighs swung wide apart as she felt the knob of his penis tickling against the lips of her vagina. She gripped both his shoulders very tightly with her hands which quivered with emotion.

Cesare wriggled on her, longing to plunge in but enjoying the sight and sound of her passion and desire.

He felt her release a shoulder and then her hand came down under her thigh and felt for and found his penis. She held it gently, seeming to hold her breath, too, at the same time, and guided it at her wide-open cunt.

Right, now, at last, Cesare thought in a sudden, fierce, violent joy. He thrust in with a long, excruciating grind, all the way in one long, agonizing movement. She drew up her thighs with his penetration and her hands bit into his shoulders.

'Aaaaaah!' The ecstatic groan dragged out from between their lips at the same moment. With her it continued on a slightly lower key, a continuous, gentle, lost groaning. With Cesare it broke down into a shunting accompaniment of groans and pantings for breath as he drove in and in, crashing and plundering, right to the soft, giving wall of the cavern's roof.

Her thighs which had opened, giving him wider access, and moved back toward her shoulders giving him depth, came down and clasped his hips, moving and slithering against them as he pistoned in and out. Her breasts flattened and rounded under his varying pressure and her eyes opened to look with abandon into his as her groaning lips sought to touch, to bite, to kiss his face, any part of his face.

His loins aflame, consumed in the ecstatic relief of her moist, claiming containment, Cesare felt her passage plucking sensation from his prick along its whole length. Her channel fitted him like a glove, smooth and with a gentle pressure which became stronger as the tip of his organ coursed right through to its end.

Already he could feel pressure building up in his pulsating staff. All that preliminary titivating had prepared his prick for a quick release.

Under him, squirming and mouthing noises, the gypsy girl, too, was building up to the intense final pressure. Her arms moved around him, over his shoulder, down his back, to his buttocks which she could just reach. She pressed on them exhorting him into her and her legs swung up suddenly and entwined his thighs and then up further and gripped his waist.

Cesare slipped his hand under her full, soft buttocks which strained down firmly in his hands and then relaxed, soft again. He reached underneath, feeling her thighs from behind and she gasped anew as his fingers entered the long slit of her vagina, pulling the lips gently apart, brushing in with his hard length of penis.

Her head began to move from side to side on the divan. Her legs released his waist and swung down, flattening into the couch and then gripped him again before falling away, almost at right angles to her body.

Her crotch was running with moisture. Cesare's fingers slipped from it and ran up the crease between her buttocks. He pulled the buttocks apart and she gave a start of passion through her moaning. He plunged a finger against the tight, warm, puckering of her anus and felt it give and his fingertip break through to soft, tender flesh.

'Oh, oh, oh!' she gasped again and again.

She began to writhe as if in a paroxysm. It must be now, Cesare was able to think as he drummed into her, pulling back and then thrusting in his whole length in a slow, grinding crush.

She opened her eyes and looked at him desperately. Her eyes seemed to be speaking to him, loving him, wanting him, abandoning herself to him. Her mouth opened and her tongue came out—a long, point-tipped, moist and perfectly smooth tongue. Cesare lowered his lips to hers and bit the tongue gently. He ground in with slow, strong strokes. He could feel his penis swelling in a hot tingling expansion. He couldn't keep his mouth on hers and drew up, his hands under her buttocks, pulling them up off the divan, against his loins.

She wriggled furiously, her shoulders quivered, and her breasts under his eyes. She groaned and looked at his eyes in a last gleam of passion and then her mouth opened in a great circle, her head dropped back, her thighs clasped him and she emitted a loud, aching gasp and another and another, dwindling away into body-racking sighs.

Still holding her buttocks in his hands, fired by the sight of her fulfilment. Cesare, himself, trembled on the brink of release. His penis was chafing against the flesh of her passage and his loins were screwed up in a turmoil of pre-explosion. Her beautiful body, heaving with passionate sighs, was in his hands. He looked down and saw her thighs hanging over his hands as he held her bottom, and saw his prick, inflamed and wet, disappearing into her red, loose lips. Her breasts swayed and heaved below him and that narrow waist was heaving too, above the hips that he held up slightly off the bed.

He thrust savagely in and felt his knob growing and growing as if it would burst into a thousand pieces. He ground slowly, slowly, extracting every iota of sensation from the long, slow stroke. His breath was rising up from his chest, rising up through his throat at the same time that his knob was expanding in unbearable torture. He felt the quick fire dart in his loins and come racing through. His mouth opened wide as the breath finally, suddenly, reached it. He shattered his sperm up, up into her belly as the breath broke from his throat, twisting his mouth out into an agonized explosion. He felt the pressure of her thighs renewed, fleetingly, heard a faint gasp echoing a recognition of his orgasm.

For several seconds he pumped into her, seeming to loose all the juices of his pent up body into that lovely, waiting receptacle. Then, slowly he collapsed on her warm, cushioning flesh and felt her arms encircle him gently and her lips, light and tender on his cheek.

Later, nude still, she preceded him as they walked to the private chamber Cesare had been allotted off the banquet hall. Watching her buttocks swaying and rounding under the slim, taut waist, Cesare wondered if the Chief Councillor meant it when he said it would be worth getting a stiletto in one's ribs if one could be sure of fulfilment first. Looking at her thighs, slenderly moving under the rounded voluptuousness of the buttocks, he felt pretty sure he meant it.

The Joys of Lolotte

**Translated from the French by
Frank Pomeranz**

The evening, though seeming like eternity, passed pleasantly enough. At supper, which was served in our rooms, I ate with gusto. My mother said she had to write a good many letters that evening. I was terrified lest she stayed up part of the night, which sometimes happened, but Félicité, with no less foresight, had seen to that. She found a way of telling me about it and laying at rest a worry that she evidently shared with me.

'Don't worry,' she said. 'I have added a reasonable dose of Madame's sleeping draught to her wine. I assure you she will quickly drop off over her writing paper and feel the need to go to bed.'

Her strategem worked as it was meant to. My mother had been at work for scarcely half an hour when, yawning, abstracted and overcome with sleep, she rang for Félicité to help her undress.

'Really,' she said to her lady's maid. 'I feel quite tipsy. It can't be what I drank at supper. It must be an excess of happiness—a sentiment that my heart has become unaccustomed to lately.'

'Happiness no doubt has something to do with it,' the cunning Félicité replied. 'But, without noticing, Madam also drank rather more than usual tonight.'

'I don't believe so.'

'I was surprised myself but Madam lightly drank off a second carafe of wine.' (This was quite untrue.)

'Is that really so?'

'I assure you, madam. Anyway, have a good rest.'

'I am so sleepy I can hardly keep my eyes open; good night, Félicité.'

'Good night, Madam.' She drew the curtains. 'I wish you happy dreams. We, too—believe me—are going to have a good night after the happy events of the day.'

'I hope so, my children.'

'Good night, Mother.'

'Good night, Madam.'

We still had an hour to ourselves. Lord, how slowly the time passed. I was terribly impatient. Leaping from my seat to the window every few moments like a squirrel, I got even more tired and restless; by turns, I questioned Félicité, called her names and even hit her because she said, though with a laugh, that perhaps instead of expecting a man, we should prepare ourselves to discover that the idea of an assignation was the treacherous trick of some wicked hussy trying to compromise us with my mother and the Mother Superior.

At heart, however, Félicité, who was able to control herself better than I, was no less hopeful; what she said was merely to rein in my petulance a little and to give herself the mischievous pleasure of contradicting me.

But, in the end, when I went to the window for perhaps the hundredth time, what joy! I caught a glimpse of something moving in the garden . . . the object came closer; I called Félicité over. . . . First we saw a figure, then a ladder approaching our window. . . . How my heart was beating!

The ladder was put in position; the figure moved away and then returned. Good grief! It was . . . it was . . . only a nun! All at once my blood ran cold and fury replaced hope and desire. It would not have needed much for me to push over the ladder and hurl it, together with the figure on it, into the garden.

How unjust a person can be and how blameworthy if he acts rashly. How dreadful it would have been if I had been the cause of the charming creature that was coming to call on us breaking its neck.

The habit was straightaway cast off by our gentleman visitor (for it turned out that he really was male): ardent caresses were at once bestowed impartially on the mistress and servant.

'You understand, of course, my darlings, that midnight rendez-vous in a nunnery are not made for sentimental romances. More than once I have overheard your intimate conversations and listened to your discussions. I know full well what you think and what you desire and I shall supply what you need.'

We had already had our bodices and skirts removed, because his hands had not lagged behind his speech in carrying negotiations forward. What an expert undresser of girls he was, to be sure!

'Let's get to work quickly and jointly. Let's shut the windows, draw the curtains and shade the lights. Let's not stand on ceremony and let us drop all inhibitions.'

At this point my shift was removed; I was immediately seized below my buttocks and lifted up so that my downed *honey-pot* could be freely kissed. I was released; now it was Félicité's turn and her magnificent breasts were gratified by the most ardent caresses. My own, alas, had not been treated like that—there was still too little of them. Now he returned to me. I was carried to the bed. At the same moment, Félicité's shift dropped to her feet. The hussy knew full well to what extent the advantageous display of her many charms would redound to her credit. The young man's reaction was striking—like that of Pygmalion prostrating himself at the feet of his Galathea taking her first breath. Félicité was hugged, covered with kisses all over—literally all over—and laid on the bed beside me. At almost the same moment, the young man was as stark naked as we were ourselves. But for the absence of wings, he was an angel or rather as one would imagine Apollo or Belvedere but with a *prick*! Heavens, what a *prick*! It was the first I had ever seen in the flesh and, alas, I have never had the good fortune to see another like it.

Imagine the embarrassment of a young worshipper, burning with desire, about to offer up his sacrifice, who has at his mercy on the altar two victims, one of whom is only a servant but mature, ravishing and perfectly made for enjoyment, whereas the other is her mistress but a mere sketch of a future masterpiece, having little to set against the charms of her attractive rival apart from the fantastic advantage of her virginity. While it is known that the latter is a powerful bait for many gallants, there are a great many others whom it does not interest in the slightest: the true man of pleasure attaches little value to the specious pleasures of self-esteem. So I had no reason to think that if the choice between us had been perfectly free the scales would have come down in my favour.

Félicité, it must be said, did nothing to persuade him that she should be awarded the apple, because I seemed to desire it so much, too much perhaps. The role of my inferior, my domestic servant, was to discourage both the young man and myself from follies which—while we were together—she could tolerate but which could still be avoided as long as a shred of principle could still set limits to my fiery desires. The role of the Adonis was to avoid humiliating either of us; mine ought to have been not to demand so transparently, by my looks and attitude, that the flame that was progressively consuming me should at last be extinguished.

I wanted it so much; yet, I did not. I wanted to brave whatever might be coming to me; yet, I was afraid. The brat who had set her mind on being penetrated and had imagined that in her furious desire she would be capable of seizing the first hobbledehoy who came her way by the trousers—this foolish creature, I say, became increasingly reluctant as luck appeared to favour her more and more.

Let us cut a long story short. Félicité, lightly passed over, was neglected in my favour. The angel of pleasure, covering me with his heavenly body, said to me,

'Us two first, my little darling. For the first time, I can't promise you much joy. But I hope soon and often to reward you for the pleasure you will give me. Kiss me.'

What transports and what fire I put into that kiss, which was my only response!

'All the same, ask yourself,' he said after touching my little crack, 'will your miniature charms be able to sustain the rough assault of this, which is out of all proportion to them?'

I had seized it and my hand was scarcely able to encompass it: it was long in proportion, hard and hot.

'Shall we put it in?'

'Oh yes, please do,' I replied, throwing all caution to the winds. 'Do your best, sir, come what may.'

'She wants it,' he said smiling at Félicité.

'You're going to kill her,' she replied. 'Hold on a minute; I'll preside over this dangerous operation; let me do it, I'll direct it myself. Good heavens, what an enormous thing! No, Mademoiselle, with your sixteen years and your eye of a needle you'll never accommodate this enormous fellow.'

'Just go on, my dear, do your best.'

After that, the happy young man gave her free rein to do what she wanted. He was preoccupied with my kisses which stoked his fires and submitted to the attentions of the maid who, after applying the whole of a pot of cold cream to our playthings, finally placed the enormous button against the narrow button-hole. But in vain did she hold it open, in vain did she strangle the glans of the enormous *prick* in its hood to make it more pointed; she could not make it penetrate even a fraction of an inch.

He pushed; I lunged against him—but it was all to no avail. Our conjunction proved impossible.

But still, you cannot with impunity for long have your lips glued to those of a charming girl, with your *prick* in the hands of another beauty and rubbing against a maidenhead. As a result of these delicious experiences, the electric current of pleasure could not fail to affect the young man and a torrent of hot *spunk* gushed forth. Félicité believed that a joint effort, aided by the life-giving fluid, would at last break down the barrier.

'Push, my children. It must go in—now or never.'

We pushed hard enough to do ourselves a grievous

injury. All in vain. The precious ejaculation occurred entirely outside me and I was not even broached.

'Fate is cruel,' my young man said calmly as he changed position, 'but just regard it as a postponed fixture. I know precisely, my little darling, what you need; tomorrow—without fail—there are going to be two of us and you shall have what you need. And that contumaceous maidenhead will give way, I promise.'

He was still speaking to me when he was already mounted on Félicité and attacking her most sensitive spot. She was surprised—or pretending to be—at this abrupt transition and wanted a little more ceremony—but he would have none of it.

'What, in front of Mademoiselle?', the hypocritical hussy said when it was almost too late, 'at least wait till I snuff out the candles; she must not watch this infamy.'

'God damme, if this were a public square, at noon, in front of the queen, I wouldn't let go of any part of you.'

'Quite right,' I interrupted, putting on a brave face in spite of my misfortune, though I was still a little out of countenance on account of the game with me having been abandoned so quickly.

To console myself a little at least. I feasted my eyes on the majestic entry of this beautiful *prick* into the maid's receptive and docile sheath. How could I possibly have borne anything of such dimensions! Even she made a bit of a face but every heave of her hips and haunches made another good inch of the formidable cylinder disappear and before long I saw both brave champions engaged, so to speak, skin to skin.

Tell me frankly what you think, true lovers and knowledgeable connoisseurs of all things voluptuous.

Is there anything on earth so fine, so admirable and so exciting as the sight of two perfect bodies being united by the introduction of a *prick*, bursting with health, into a *cunt* palpitating with lust? This ivory, this lily, these roses, this ebony, or this gold, all moving, colliding, struggling ... what a spectacle for the gods! They have made the eyes of the vulgar multitude chary of looking on while such things go on in order that they might enjoy them in privacy. But the elite of us mortals is made to share the sublime pleasure of those directly taking part. Everyone who *fucks* is a base ingrate if he does not in his heart have the ardent desire to let others watch what he himself does with such delight.

What you have missed, gentle reader, is not seeing, like me, the superb Félicité moaning with pleasure and rocking with her gentle movements the demi-god tumbling about on top of her! Oh, how inadequate this description is compared with the most beautiful scene of *fucking* that the human mind can conceive!

Not only did I not want to miss the most insignificant detail that my avid eyes could see; I also had to grope above and below—in all directions. I admired the almost chilly spheres in the element of fire surrounding them, contained in their elastic, wrinkled bag, which at one moment rubbed against the lower corner of the *cunt* and the next, separated from it by the entire length of the *prick*, the ridge of which almost appeared outside, as if to impress me with the adroitness with which it immediately re-sheathed itself up to the very *balls*. What grace, what harmony there was in the vigorous work of these two expert creatures!

By accident, I created for myself a small part in this voluptuous scene and my success in it made me quite proud. My fingers, lightly walking over the buttocks, thighs and genitalia of this Adonis appeared to give him great pleasure; nor was I niggardly in my stimulating attentions when I realized how much he enjoyed them.

'Oh, yes! Like that,' he said. 'Go on tickling, my little darling; tickle them well; one day they will amply repay you for what you are doing now.'

By degrees, Félicité warmed to her task. 'I am going to come but if you come at the same time, I'll be lost: we are more likely to make two babies than one. Can you slow down a bit?'

'I'll see to everything, don't worry.'

'Your word of honour?'

'You have it.'

'All right, then.'

At this point her movements became awesomely agitated and now she did everything herself.

'Give me your lips, my lover. Kiss me, my angel! Oh, my God! What a glorious *fuck*!'

This sacred word was followed by silence, enforced by the fury of the kiss by which she held her lover's entire mouth engulfed in hers. She gathered him to herself by the arms and legs and held him close, trembling. This ecstatic state lasted a good two minutes; it continued even when all her limbs weakened and the prisoner at last regained his freedom. He used it at once to accomplish his own task. A moment of the same ardour that had been displayed by Félicité now brought him to his crisis. She, immobile, her arms spread out, her head turned on one shoulder and as if in a faint, took no notice of anything. All the same, true to his word, the happy young man did not fail to withdraw at the decisive moment. The thick fleece of the maid was liberally sprinkled but I observed that the unction, now more limpid, flowed less freely than earlier on with me. The beautiful young man's kept promise was rewarded with the tenderest of caresses. Now we washed; all three of us needed to badly. Félicité tidied up the bed a little and we warmed ourselves up in it, putting the dear creature who had just worked so well for our happiness in the middle.

Who was he? We were dying to know. But our curiosity was not to be satisfied yet.

Don't worry, my children.' he told us. 'One day I shall be able to tell you by what chance I became the spoilt child of this nunnery, in which—to be sure—I have many clients beside yourselves.'

'Would you believe it?'

'I cannot tell you more at the moment; but you should know that here, my dear children, you are more or less . . . in a brothel and that at this very moment there are six or seven males scattered about the sleeping quarters of this nunnery. There is apparently a god for fornicators and this god gives his special protection to a community so fervent in its worship of him; all the same, so much blatant scandal goes on here that one day—possibly quite soon—all this *fucking* may blow up in our faces.'

I suddenly had an idea. If, as he said, there really were six or seven males scattered about the sleeping quarters at that moment, would it not be possible to look for one more suitably built for my requirements, who could deputize for our visitor . . . I wanted to convey this thought to Félicité at once, so I asked our lover to raise himself slightly to enable me to whisper this lubricious thought in her ear.

'What a randy devil you are,' the malicious maid cried out aloud. 'Do you think the nuns have less of an appetite than you and are going to take the titbit out of their own mouths to feed you? And do you expect Monsieur to go out pimping for you? That, assuredly, is too much to expect of our gallant.'

'How delicious she is,' he said, hugging me. 'I don't think it's too much to ask at all. I'd be honoured to take the job on. Oh, my little darling, what a great name you'll soon be making for yourself in the world of *fucking*. I already regard you as one destined to take the blue riband of fornication and I already adore you on that account. What a pity, though' he added, 'that it won't be me . . .' (at this point he passed his hand over my little *cunt*) 'no, it's impossible.'

'Alas, what a dreadful shame!' I replied and sought out his monstrous engine. I surprised it at rest and in the shape of a swan's neck. But like a sleeping snake inadvertently touched by the heel of a huntsman, it no sooner felt the touch of my curious hand than it proudly raised its head and immediately recovered its old majesty. This made me sigh even more sadly, 'Oh, what a great shame.'

'Well, as for me,' Félicité, who was now caressing it as well, butted in gaily, 'I found it so good that if it had been any less long, or stiff or hot, I would have said even more fervently than you two: "Oh, what a shame!" '

'I've got something quite amusing to suggest,' our charming friend, whom our conversation had made randy again, said, 'which would occupy the two of you very pleasurably for a quarter of an hour.'

'Both of us?' I exclaimed with pleasure. 'Ah, my love, do tell us how.'

'I'll stay where I am' (he was on his back) 'and the charming maid will kindly sit astride me facing the foot of the bed . . . Yes, that's it' (Félicité was already mounting him) ' . . . she will be so good as to put it up her. Ah, lovely! At the same time, the little one will also bestride me facing in the same direction . . . yes, that's it and yield her pretty bottom to my observation and her little *cunt* to my kisses . . . marvellous!'

His suggestions were carried out as he made them. How readily a man is obeyed when it is pleasure he orders!

Félicité already had him up her, up to his *balls*; my *quim*, made more sensitive by our fruitless attempt earlier, was lightly moving round the loving tongue of the Adonis . . . Oh, ye gods! What charm the magnet of sex added to gamahouching, with which, of course, I was already familiar from my sessions with Félicité. What a surfeit of joy I felt when I allowed my hands to wander round the perfect hips and *arse* of the lucky maid, seeing her rise and subside rhythmically the better to be rammed by the full length of that magnificent engine. What a moment it was when he and the two of us, electrified to the very marrow of our bones, commingled the sounds of our luxurious agony!

But, above all, what a piquant variation was introduced by Félicité's whim when, finishing first, she did not think only of her own happiness and for a moment liberated this great *prick* which she had inundated with her own *cunt-juice* and at once enslaved it again more narrowly two inches away. From the very first stroke, it felt at home in the new scabbard and was able to run its course there.

'Come, my master, 'Félicité said passionately. '*Fuck*

your Félicité in the *arse* like this, *bugger* her for all you're worth. Give her all you have. In this hole there's nothing to fear. It can safely lap up all your heavenly *spunk*.

I saw her make an effort to get penetrated deeper still and her attempt was happily crowned with success.

Our jolly friend evidently had nothing against this form of pleasure because he intensified his action with his mistress and, as for me, I felt myself being *sucked off* with greater vigour. After some time, we both swooned. Félicité, duly charged and discharged, drooped forwards, her face against the feet of her lover, whose syringe was still active and spreading its drug.

But already this once so proud *prick* was losing its noble countenance. I touched it and separated it from the impure orifice in which it was lodged. It now resembled a flower which a fresh breeze had made sway in the air, its head now this way, now that; all the same it still fascinated me. Had it not just emerged from so questionable a place, how much I should have liked to kiss it.

The self-esteem of a gentleman of quality will not allow him to prolong a scene which is beginning to drag. So, our hero (no longer as heroic as before) got up almost immediately and donned his nun's habit again. Then, having promised without fail to come back next day *accompanied by a friend of the appropriate size for me*, he returned to his ladder and withdrew as happy as a sand-boy. We congratulated ourselves on having enjoyed so much pleasure with so little trouble. But our senses were sated, our eyelids drooping and we soon fell into the most profound sleep.

The Memoirs of
Madame
Madelaine

New York! Mecca toward which every country girl in America turns her face or her heart! City of fabulous wealth and untold poverty. City of exquisite refinements and gross depravities, of churches and bawdyhouses, of wide streets and narrow souls. In brief, a city of contrasts and contradictions. Anyway, this was the year 1907—a long time ago. Perhaps things have changed since then.

New Year's Eve Charley and a number of the boys were going on what they designated a 'slumming cruise' and I was invited to come along. As the party contemplated touching on some rather rough places, and the company of a woman might cause embarrassment, it was devised that I should masquerade as a man. Each had some bit of masculine haberdashery to contribute.

All in all, I made up rather successfully as an attractive, though slightly hothouse-grown young man. The greatest problem was the disposal of my long, thick hair, which I thought I could conceal but temporarily beneath a soft checkered cap. I was assured, however, that at the places we were going to visit, gentlemen did not remove their hats—or rather, there would be no gentlemen.

I even spent some time practising to speak in a lower register. My voice being naturally somewhat strong, this was not difficult. Yet at times I struck tones that were much too musical to pass for other than those of a Priscilla or a 'pansy'.

That evening was a haze of tobacco smoke and alcoholic fumes, a succession of fancy and cheap cabarets, with their corresponding demi-mondaine habitués, a medley of shouts, songs and tooting horns, with sex stories presenting a continual obligato.

At about 1 a.m. we were encamped in a somewhat quieter type of rendezvous, where the great number of unescorted ladies—and more particularly their boudoir costumes—made it obvious that drinks and music were not the only commodities for sale here.

No sooner were we all seated at a large corner table than a number of these ladies gathered about us. I was surprised to note that many of them were astonishingly good-looking and all had some considerable fund of bodily charm. The slight contempt that I had had for men who patronized prostitutes vanished immediately. Somehow I had always felt that only those women who were insufficiently attractive to ensnare permanent mates ever resorted to this profession. But now, with this proof positive before me, it seemed more likely that only those whose charms were too slight to insure numerous successive admirers would steer for the safe harbour of marriage with its stagnant waters. True, some of them seemed rather hard, vulgar specimens. But marriage is more likely to contain great numbers of viragos than this profession whose purpose is to please—and I was beginning to learn that there are degrees of refinement even among the votaries of Venus Pandemos.

One of their number, the youngest by appearance, singled me out for her especial attention. My embarrassment could be better imagined than described—particularly, when my companions, realizing the humour of the situation, urged her on to overcome my 'bashfulness'.

The lady in question was a delightful young thing of about my age and size, with titian-red hair and eyes of a strange dark blue that bordered on green. Beneath the diaphanous black silk combination, that was all that she wore, could be discerned the pink-white prominences of her pretty form, the firm tract of her belly and a pair of pert, luscious breasts that seemed so deliciously edible that even I, who should have felt a minimum of response to such charms, experienced a deep impulse to bite into them—just to feel those tiny cherry nipples upon the back of my tongue with the surrounding ivory flesh caressing my lips. Her thighs and legs, though they demanded less attention by very reason of the fact that they were entirely bare except for the uppermost segments, were as shapely as any I had seen. A string of jade beads and a pair of tiny scarlet slippers completed her clothed protection—and little enough it was.

Sitting beside me on the wall-seat, she made herself agreeable to me in what I supposed was the conventional manner.

'You are a very handsome boy,' she said, with a slight accent that I immediately surmised as French, running her fingertips in a peculiarly subtle manner up my thighs. 'You would make a very pretty girl,' I winced, but smiled at her in lieu of the words I dared not speak.

'But I like you,' she went on. 'Do you wish to kiss me?' I shook my head. 'No? You're afraid of me? Come now, I won't bite you. Give me your arm. Now—put it around my waist, so. And your hand—here. Like that? Nice, isn't it? Make you feel like doing anything? No? Then your other hand.' She pursed her pretty red lips patiently. 'Put it here on my thigh, so. You like that? Nice and warm, isn't it? Well, *do* something!' This time with a tiny trace of exasperation. 'I'm not your maiden aunt. You can move your hands a little bit. I won't slap you.'

Complying, I closed one hand over the firm little hillock of one of her bosoms, while with the fingers of the other hand that lay in her lap, I felt timidly about, sensing, through the silk of her combination, the crisp tiny clump of pubic hairs that rustled at my touch. Simultaneously, her deft, naughty little hand crept up my trousered thigh again to my corresponding part, feeling about for the expected result in vain. Of necessity, the phenomenon she desired was impossible; but little did she suspect that the strangeness of the situation was arousing me more than her caresses alone could affect any mere man. And if a penis had been the indicator of my suppressed excitement, I am certain it would have burst every last button on those borrowed trousers I wore.

But finding no index to my state, and therefore, reasonably deeming it a mark of her insufficiency, Nanette (for that was her name) pushed my hands from her, much to my regret, and spoke petulantly.

'You don't like me! I am too ugly for you perhaps. You want me to leave you and send one of the other girls?'

'No, no! I like you,' I ventured to say in low tones that were fortunately made hoarse by my sensual commotion. Whether the assumption of male clothes had worked a sexual transformation within me and my feelings were those of a man for a woman, or whether I had brought to light a heretofore concealed homosexual tendency or not, I cannot say. A simpler explanation would be that the presence of anything associated with sexual pleasure—and lord knows this creature's every curve and fold spoke only of the extremest sensual ecstasies—would stimulate male or female alike, by being interpreted associatively either actively or passively, as the case might be. 'I would like to fuck her' or 'I would like to be her when she gets fucked' is the idea.

Whatsoever the reason though—and too much reasoning is inimical to joy, I must remind myself again and again—I was anxious lest I lose the company of this luscious girlie, and forgetting myself completely, threw my arms about her neck and placed on her mouth a fierce, salacious kiss. I was pleased to find that her ripe moist lips were fresh and sweet, with that vague ambrosial perfume that women can give but cannot receive in kissing a man—and I was not averse when she prolonged the delicious contact by introducing the scarlet tip of her tiny tongue into my mouth. I am not idly employing metaphors when I write that during those few fervid moments my very heart sprang to my lips.

It was only after this compromising admission that I became aware that my companions, though they had been occupying only the periphery of my consciousness, had focused on me at least half their entire attention. They were nudging each other and laughing delightedly at my performance, not for a moment dreaming that it had not been entirely unwilling.

'Would you like to come upstairs with me, dearie?' Nanette whispered when she noted how discomfited I was by the onlookers. I shook my head negatively.

'Would you like to take me home with you then?'
I shook my head again.

'Then we can spend the night together at a hotel.
I will be so very nice to you. Everything. Yes?'

Again I shook my head. By this time, the boys
gathered from my repeated 'no's' the way the land
lay, and considering it a rare joke, boisterously gave
aid to her cause, urging me to go upstairs with her.

'Go ahead, Lou. She'll make a man of you!' Such
were the jibes cast at me. At last, to put a stop to this
roistering, which already was attracting the attention
of all present, and to spare the little lady the public
insult that my continued refusal would now be, I
nodded my head in assent. She took my hand happily
and led me away; but not without my turning back
to give my blackest look to my companions for
subjecting me to this unspeakable embarrassment.

At a sort of office in the rear, Nanette was thrown
a towel and a key—much like the procedure of renting
a bathouse at our beaches—and I was handed,
imagine, a rubber sheath. Instantly falling out of role,
I threw the condom back and continued on. My petulance drew only a polite smile from the madam and
an 'As you will, sir.'

On the stairs, I decided it was time to disclose my
real sex and bring to a close this comedy of errors. I
tapped Nanette on the shoulder and stopped halfway
up; but somehow, the words I would have spoken did
not come. Perhaps the strange excitement, or fear of
an emotional outbreak on her part, or perhaps curiosity as to the outcome, inhibited me. She merely took
me by the hand once more and dragged me on, saying.
'Don't be afraid, child. It'll do you a lot of good. And
you'll be glad you came. I like it too. For my sake

171

you will do it; because you are a very nice boy and already I love you.'

We entered a brightly lit but plainly furnished room and the key was turned in the lock. Against the wall was a large heavy bed with fresh white linens. Over the lowermost part of the sheets, however, was spread a strip of dark blanketing—probably as a footrest for those who didn't stay long enough to remove their shoes.

'Now we are alone, honey,' Nanette addressed me as I continued to stand near the door. She approached, embraced me tightly, and rolling her waist and hips against my middle with a tense, slow movement that once more made me regret that I possessed no more projectible antenna with which to savour this contact, she placed a long hot kiss upon my mouth. I returned it with sudden, abandoned fervour.

She stepped away from me. A slight shake of her body, and the flimsy black silk under-garment that had been her sole costume slipped down from off her shoulders till only the upstanding heights of her breasts sustained it; another motion, and it slipped down to the station of her full wide hips; another, and the cloud of silk glided shyly down her thighs and settled slowly about her tiny slippered feet.

There she stood before me, nude—an apparition of beauty that not even Chrysis of old could have surpassed when she disrobed for some burning, handsome lover in the moonlit groves behind the temple of Aphrodite.

What divine flesh! How lovely a form! I would have envied her inconsolably, had not the thought flashed upon me that I could not have loved that gorgeous body one half so passionately, so desirously, if it had been my own. From her gracious neck to her swelling, rounded young breasts my gaze went to the snowy valley between that widened downward to the broad delicious plain of her belly; the dimpled navel; the well-shaded triangular patch, overspread with curling silken hair of the richest, sable—beneath which began a scarcely discernible rift that shaded modestly down and inward to seek shelter between two plump fleshy thighs of just that proportion which is not too much for grace and yet enough for love's luscious demands.

A moment she stood for my admiration, then turning away, presented to my intoxicated view less consciously, another side that put me in deep quandary as to which, front or back, was the more beautiful. The rear of her thighs, more curved, more fleshy, more lascivious than the front, where, in close conjunction they plumped out in a pair of the most delicious white buttocks conceivable, would have stricken dead with desire any sodomist worshipper of Venus Callipyge.

Briskly, and to reassure the fearful young man that I still was to her, she bent over a sort of *bidet pour abolutions intimes*, and with an apologetic smile to me, proceeded to quickly soap and wash her private parts. Grotesque as this action may have been in reality, yet it in no way interrupted or dispelled the tense atmosphere of desire that enwrapped me. On the contrary, if I had been a man with all that belongs to a man, so inflamed by her suggestive squatting position would I have been, that I would have rushed upon her and impaled her soap and all, then and there!

Humming a little tune and watching me intently,

she gently dried herself with the towel, leaving her pubic hairs more silky, more curly and delightfully tousled than ever. Then, throwing herself on her back across the bed, she drew up her legs, spread wide her thighs and awaited me.

Irresistibly I was drawn near. The fascination of the vista spread before me held me breathless with a strange wild pleasure. Through the dark silky curls of her mount of Venus could be seen, like the setting sun through foliage, the merest suggestion of vermilion. And beneath that, the veritable red-centred velvety cleft of flesh itself, with its soft lovely little lips, shading gradually inward from palest pink through intermediate delicate tones of red to deepest carmine—expressing a harmony of line and colour, of softness and vividness, that Renoir at his best has never attained.

But alas! I could do not more than gaze upon it. Nature had sadly failed to bless me with the wherewithal to give that darling cunny that which it pouted for.

For a while the adorable creature continued in her expectant attitude. At last, seeing that not only had I not made proper application of the essential specific, but had not yet even disclosed it, she sat up on the edge of the bed and sighed patiently.

'Still bashful, eh? Well, come sit beside me. Either you've had too much of women or none at all. Which is it? Are you a virgin?'

I nodded affirmatively. All too truly.

'Well, well. I should feel honoured. You are my first beginner. But I thought nature would take care of herself and tell you what to do. Come closer. Put your arms around me. Now play with me while I get you ready.'

She bit her lower lip, and with a pretty little frown of earnestness, began studiously to attack the front buttons of my trousers. I was mortified beyond words. What could I say, after leading her on so far? I could only await the inevitable.

The last button was opened. Her pretty little hand insinuated itself into the gap with becoming awkwardness, felt about with increasing anxiety for the stiff bar of flesh, the male *ne plus ultra*, that should have sprung to her grasp, but was not there.

Instead she encountered only the soft silk of the feminine underthings I had retained despite my disguise. Grope as she might, there was not even the meagerest suspicion of the affirmative intrument she was no doubt sufficiently acquainted with to certify the absence of.

'Mother of God!' she exclaimed in horror, rapidly making the sign of the cross over her nude bosom. 'What kind of man are you? Have you been castrated? Were you born this way? And those silk underclothes—Ugh!'

I could only hang my head in shame.

'Why don't you answer me?' she went on. 'Are you deaf and dumb too? Why do you come here to waste a poor girl's time, you—you dirty catamite!' And she slapped me sharply across the cheek.

Still I could not articulate a sound. Bursting into tears of discomfiture and shame, my head still hung low, I pulled off the cap that till now I had kept jealously on my head. The loosely piled up tresses of my hair tumbled about my face and bosom like a shower of autumn leaves.

'Good Jesus, help me!' exclaimed the pious Nanette in amazement at this denouement. 'A woman! Or can it be a further deception of the devil?'

'No—a woman.' I spoke for the first time. Still sceptical, the good Nanette, with native directness, whipped down my already fully opened trousers, and searched through the tangle of my silk chemise till she found the conclusive proof of my statement.

Laughing delightfully now, with relief and appreciation for the jest, she placed a kiss on the bare smooth skin of my thigh, a quick little kiss that set us both blushing furiously.

'And a very pretty woman, too. My faith—but you surely fooled me.' She was looking me up and down, her eyes ever glistening and dancing with interest. 'But I don't care. I'd rather you were a woman anyway. I don't like men. They're just my business. But you—there was something about you that I liked from the beginning.'

Her bright smile was irresistible. 'You too, Nanette; there was something about you that made me really almost fall in love with you. Even now I wish I were a man.'

For the first time in that whole hectic evening I felt happy and released from the strain of carrying on my pretence. Kicking the trousers off from my ankles, I lay back upon the soft bed.

'Why don't you take those stiff ugly clothes off, dearie?' Nanette suggested. 'You've only been up here a few minutes. Your friends are probably busy with the other women and have forgotten all about you.'

I complied, while she considerately helped me off with the now hateful coat, vest, shirt and heavy shoes.

In a moment I was lying comfortably on the bed with nothing on but a pale green silk chemise.

'You are built beautifully,' Nanette said in low, admiring tones. I returned a similar compliment, but she ignored it, engrossed only in me.

'Your breasts are so full and rounded,' she went on. 'How did you ever keep them out of sight without a corset? They must be much softer and more compressible than mine. Mine are hard and firm. Feel.' And she led my hand to one of her globes of ivory, which may have been firm, but hard, never.

'Do you care if I touch yours?' she asked now, rather anxiously. I assented.

To complete her comparison, she gently slipped my chemise down off my bosom to my very hips—and then, suddenly abandoning the pretext of polite conversation, she threw herself upon me, fondling, kissing and biting my breasts with the fierce ardour of a lover and murmuring, 'I love you! I love you!'

The strange, perhaps abnormal, emotion, the merest suggestions of which I had felt before, now flamed forth in an overwhelming fever that must have out-temperatured Nanette's hot lips at every point where they met my flesh. My will melted away. I lay, grateful and passive to her caresses. Vaguely, I wondered at the forceful affirmativeness of her passion; as for myself, I still felt only deliciously feminine—although in my consciousness a gathering undertone insisted on mad, wild pleasures, the more forbidden, the more perverted, the more blasphemous to codes of man or God, the better!

My Nanette was leaning over my outstretched form at right angles to it, thus giving herself access to every part of me. Using her hands no more than if she had

had none, she continued covering me with hot kisses. Now she leaves off sucking my nipples to tongue the tiny ticklish depression of my navel, leaving a path of deliciously wet kisses in her wake.

On every exposed part of my body her lips worship. Now she is venturing lower to my hips. At this extra-sensitive zone her kisses cause my abdomen to contract sharply, spasmodically, again and again.

All over my belly again and down toward my thighs her kisses trail delightfully, setting off little titillating explosions of sensation through my whole body. As she goes lower, and lower still, she pushes before her with her head the loose silk chemise that lies lightly in her path—still not deigning to use her hands. I aid her by slightly raising my hips and buttocks from the bed, and thus she drives this last flimsy garment down before her with her kisses, down every fought-for inch to my thighs, and to my very knees.

Now up my thighs, and as deeply between them as she can reach, her lips and tongue run their delicious way. Gradually, I allow her to force my legs apart. Unceasingly she kisses and bites the inviting soft white flesh of my between-thighs, closer, closer to my awakening centre.

Panting with passion, she arrives at the edge of the very spot; then, exhausted by her continual kissing, she rests, burying her face deep in that strategic area where thighs at their most luscious meet belly and mossy mound and velvety cunt.

Full upon the sensitive seat of all my sensations her hot breath comes, in panting blasts like the scalding draft of a blacksmith's bellows. Up from my vulva to my very womb the heat spreads, firing further my already burning senses to a white unendurable heat, bringing down generous vaginal secretions and lubricants that are but oil to the flames. Uncontrollable as a nervous tic, my cunny is shaken by little spasms, and my hips begin writhing about in upward spirals. I cannot long endure her inaction. I am a soul in torment.

At last my exquisite female lover resumes. Boldly her mouth seizes upon the lips of my tender cunny and places full upon it a long luscious kiss. My clitty is galvanized into quivering erectness, and I almost scream with delight. Now I know my torment is past, that this way lies ecstasy and relief—that Nanette is not simply engaging in fruitless caresses and abortive titillations.

But no. Her dear mouth abandons the vital spot that so deeply craves her attention, and goes awandering again. Heavens! Why does she torture me so? Has she found that part distasteful? Or is she merely teasing my senses with prolonged suspense?

Happily it is the latter—else surely I would have died from that excessive, stinging desire.

Her pretty ruby lips once more make the circuit of my body, everywhere stirring up nervous reactions and reflexes that I had never before so much as dreamt of.

I open my eyes, which till now have been closed, to more fully concentrate upon the universe of sensual delights within and upon the surface of my body. Nanette too, it appears, is sustaining the full lash of desire. Her whole form, though flushed with internal heat, is shivering and vibrating with a strange nervousness.

Up till now her attention is all to me. But now, as her lips once more steal downward to the home base, she brings her whole perfect nude body around and upon me, in a reverse position, not for one moment abandoning the stimulating, titllating aggravation of her mouth.

The wondrous treasure of her glowing form is now suspended over me as she supports herself, her hands on each side of my thighs, her knees bestraddling my head. For a moment I glimpse down the vista made by the quickly narrowing space between our parallel naked forms—above my quivering abdomen. And overhead, her plump white thighs, crowned at their juncture with her now widespread pouting cunny, ripe, luscious and scarlet as a freshly severed pomegranate, and padded for protection of its delicate membranes with soft, curly hairs.

Our bodies at last in contact, flesh to flesh, our breathing now becomes synchronized with the rise and fall of breasts against diaphragm and diaphragm against breasts. Nor do her lips relinquish their activity for one moment during this transaction.

Her arms now slip under and embrace my thighs to bring my middle the closer to her. A moment she reaches down to whisk my chemise from off its last post on my lower legs, and now I am free to throw my limbs wide apart. Awhile longer she circles my anxious centre with a barrage of kisses. Now her face burrows deep between my fleshy thighs, and then—good God, what ecstatic relief—her mouth seeks and finds unerringly my palpitating cunny!

A sucking kiss upon the very clitty itself makes me nearly swoon with joy. Now her tongue softly but firmly ploughs down through the whole groove of my cunt, gently parting the adhering lips and laying open new sensitive zones, new nerve cells, for her ineffably wonderful lingual caresses. What an exquisite feeling pervades all my senses! Oh, gods and men, how I pity you for not having such a deep membranous organ as a cunt with which to experience this superheavenly exquisite delight. For no prick, be it ever so large and sensitive, can have that quantity of mucous nerve-netted surface that a woman's cunt is blessed with and that makes possible such subtle sensations as the sacred ritual of the cunnilingus alone can give! Oh gods and men, I exclaim again, I would not have accepted all the wealth of ancient Carthage in exchange for that one first lapping stroke of joy-giving tongue in my cunt!

Up to this moment, though Nanette's exquisite little quim was directly overhead, the inertia of modesty had restrained me from making any overtures comparable to hers, and I had kept my head slightly averted. But now, as more rapidly her agile tongue stirs up my boiling passions below, I, in gratefulness and in plain unadulterated lasciviousness, reach up with my arms, encircle her buttocks so conveniently near, and draw her quivering coral cunt down, down toward my face, to my panting mouth, to my waiting, lolling tongue. Her soft velvety thighs settle close about my cheeks. Immediately before my eyes are the lovely swelling prominences of her buttocks, the skin, even at this close range, whiter and more flawless than I had deemed possible. Between them, her pretty little bum, puckered delightfully, of a sepia tinge that faded to pink, to white, as its harmonious ridges melted into the gracious snowdrifts of her bottom. Below, separated from it only by a narrow little partition of pink flesh, the mystic grotto of love itself, leading in, inward, to woman's most vital organs and the wondrous womb of life; but more immediately showing a perfect ellipse of the most luscious vermilion that gaped invitingly at its widest, and melted together, just the other side of a small but inescapable projection, the clitty, in a little rift that lost itself in the abundant silky shrubbery of the Hill of Venus.

I raised my mouth to this delightful valley of love. If ever I had imagined qualms or compunctions about what I was on the verge of doing, they vanished instantly. Was it Juvenal, that old smart-acre, who insinuated, 'The breath of pederasts is foul; but what of those who lick the vulva?' If so, it is because his country was bathless and his women unwashed. No doubt his own mouth, unacquainted with the tooth-brush, was nothing to write odes about. But in this modern day, a woman's personal hygiene is an accepted fact, and the vaginal cavity may be as clean or cleaner than the oral.

Nanette's delicious quim possessed only the faint wholesome, personal odour of a young and healthy woman. This was subtly blended with the artificial perfume of her adjoining parts, and the whole gave a delicate local aroma that was stimulating and inde-scribably pleasing to my senses. Avidly I breathed it in, as I plunged my tongue into the exquisite crimson cavern. The warm, moist membranes, ineffably smooth and soft, gave as much caress to my lips and mouth as I in turn gave them.

In the meantime, my beloved Nanette is by no means idle. Now deftly and rhythmically, now with the uncontrolled fury of passion, her tongue weaves in and out among the folds of my inner cunt, now straight up and down through the full length of the tender cleft, now across, now in zigzags that run from end to end, now in little circles that concentrate on my clitty and put me wholly out of my mind with unendurable pleasure, now in sweeping ovals that stir up wide rippling waves of divine ecstasy, waves that somehow spread, not in circles, but in ever-widening ellipses that take in more of my entire being.

Unconsciously, at the other end, I adopt the rhythm and actions that she employs—and all that I describe as one doing was done and felt by each and both of us. In tense pleasure, she tightens her thighs against my cheeks. Instinctively I draw up my knees from the supine position and wrap my thighs tightly about her head, thus enabling me to bring her whole beloved face in closer to my tender parts.

Now dear Nanette is moving her whole body to the rhythm of lapping tongue, rising and falling to meet every caressing stroke. Soon I am adopting the same tempo, my hips and ass writhing madly up and down to follow the fullest presence and pressure of her tongue.

Demonically inspired by passion, my teeth seize fiercely, though restrainedly, the erect palpitating little bulb of her clitoris and press firmly into it. Nanette gasps with the extremity of her pleasure; as I gently nibble the sensitive projection, I can hear her murmur in a muffled manner:

'*Ah! Mon Dieu! Que je t'aime!*' In her excitement she lapses into her native language. The sound waves, spoken directly into my cunny, send peculiar vibrations through all my bone structure.

Recovering, Nanette reciprocates in even finer measure. Opening wide her hungry mouth to encompass the whole, she sucks in with her lips and breath all the succulent folds of my cunt. Already blood-gorged and sensitive to the utmost, this action overcharges the blood vessels and nerve cells almost to the bursting point. At the same time, the vacuum made by her delicious sucking suddenly causes my whole vagina and womb to contract with a strange tingling that wrenches and cramps my entire being in an agony of delight and brings down an inundation of the sweet secretions of love as if this were already my climax. I would have screamed if I could, but Nanette's dear part hushes me with its luscious caress.

For long, deliciously agonizing moments she holds that strange mouth-suction, during which I am in no less than a state of suspended animation. Then, having wrought in that part the maximum of hyper-sensitivity possible, she suddenly releases her magic oral grip and proceeds as if to devour me with mouth, lips, tongue and teeth. A series of deep tremors shake me, so surcharged is my whole nervous system with all these kissings and teasings and bitings and suckings.

But relief is at hand: dear, desirable, delicious relief from those tortures of love, which are no sooner ended when we wish only to renew them again and again. She now ceases her hungry random attack, and with scarcely an interval, takes up with her tongue a hand to hand duel with my bounding clitoris. And with what magnificent swordsmanship! Back and forth with light but firm and ever-quickening little strokes, the sensitive tip of her tongue does battle with the even more sensitive little sentinel of my Palace of Pleasure. Not the fraction of a moment's respite does she give him. Scarcely has he rebounded, much less recovered, from one stroke than another and another and another falls to his share.

Doughty little clitty, who often enough in more common battles can vanquish and outstand in fight many a strong penis five hundred times his size—we cannot hold you to blame for your quick surrender! For what prick or clitoris, be it ever so stubborn, could long withstand that steady rain of caresses given by the moist tip of Nanette's deft, subtle tongue?

More and more rapidly the little strokes come, till the electrifying sensations that follow each come so close together as to blend into one continuous, ever-increasing, candescent ecstasy that wafts me softly skyward, as if on the magic rug of an Arabian Night's tale.

Try as I will, my own unpractised tongue cannot meet the pace she sets. And now, as the dear climax heralds its approach in my deep, violent gasps, my tongue strikes blindly, jerkily, missing strokes with every panting exhalation that is torn in sharp blasts from my writhing body. Only dear Nanette continues steadily and unflinchingly, though she too proclaims by the desperately irregular wrigglings of her buttocks that her dissolution is near.

Together now! Oh, to come together! To weld our ecstasies into one! My tongue and lips and teeth lap and kiss and bite wildly with every current of delicious pleasure that shoots through me! With difficulty I hold her madly writhing cunt to my mouth. All our universe becomes a tangle of dripping tongues and soft, warm cunt-flesh, of legs and thighs and buttocks—the whole mad scene illuminated by more and more frequent flashes of red-glowing sensation.

Suddenly, in this welter of pleasure, already superlative beyond conception, comes that infinitely superior, super-superlative of the climax!

Oh! What mortal pen can describe those divine orgasmic transports for which kingdom, life and honour are well lost? Only from the violent external manifestations can the inner turmoil be surmised. My whole body twitches in the supreme agonizing pleasure—and as the apex is reached, my thighs close so stiffly and tensely about my dear Nanette's head that I would have hurt her sadly, had not her face been cushioned by my own well-padded cunt and soft parts. As is, I crush her mouth inward to me and hold her as in a vice to put a stop to those unendurable titillations—for already my orgasm has sufficient momentum to finish of itself. But she manages to continue the fierce motion of her tongue. I am completely out of my mind! My alarmed senses scream out and struggle to retain consciousness in this turmoil of stimulations and new sensations; but despite all this, there is one obsession—to continue my own active part and to drag my companion down after me into this maelstrom of intense pleasure, to drown with me in all these swirling joys.

Madly my tongue continues lashing away, while I grip her form to me in every part. As one being now, we writhe in our embrace. Another moment, and I can tell from the sudden stiffening of her body and the sharp contraction of her cunt that she is with me! Then, and not till then, do I feel that the real apex of my own crisis is at hand.

Two long low moans go up from our tensely tangled form. First blinded, then entirely overcome, by the tremendous conflagration of sensations, I faint dead away—for long sublime moments of which, alas, I can give no report.

My joy-clouded brain begins to clear. We lie quivering and twitching in each other's arms like persons mortally stricken; but in truth we are still swimming in head-over seas of bliss. We have survived the delicious danger, and the delirium and tumult of our senses subside.

For a time we lie thus, breathless and happy, more languorously savouring the delightful afterpleasures of love. Our bodies relax, my thighs fall away from her head; Nanette's white naked form now rests upon me softly, her belly upon my breasts, a welcome blanket of gently palpitating flesh. Her cunt still lies upon my lips, but my tongue is withdrawn. As I open my eyes, till now closed in ecstasy, I can see that its folds are glowing with a more flaming vermilion than ever; but its so recently irritated membranes are now bathed and soothed by a generous flood of fine mucous. Through the vista of her still-widespread thighs and buttocks, I see the gas chandelier on the ceiling burning with what seems a dimmer flame. It is not my passion that is dimmer, however, for my mind is yet full of memories and desires for what is so recent; it is only that my eyes, their pupils contracting with languour, present the outer world thus dully in contrast to the brightness of sensation within. Oh, to lie with her forever! To sleep perhaps awhile, and then to awake to renewals of this subtle ecstasy!

Nanette is the first to stir. Much to my regret she removes her beloved body from over me and automatically resumes her dress of shoes and black silk chemise. I proceed to follow suit, but she halts my progress, covering my breasts with a round of tender kisses.

Then, full upon my mouth, still full of the dear moisture of her cunny, she places a luscious kiss.

Alternately we suck each other's lips and tongues, exchanging the sweet secretions of our mouths. As for myself, I find a deliciously wicked erotic stimulant in the thought that I am thus drinking from her lips the joint lubrications of our secret parts.

Reluctantly she begins to help me on with my clothes. Then suddenly, in a little flurry of passion, she falls to her knees as I sit on the edge of the bed and parting my thighs, she places upon the lips of my cunny what is meant as a grateful farewell kiss. Then, noting that it is still very wet, she compresses the lips together with her fingers, and leaning over it again, sucks away the moisture that she thus squeezes from it. Next, regretting the early completion of this pleasing task, she impulsively undoes her work by inserting her tongue and kissing it more moistly than ever.

Still unable to tear herself away from this most delicious part of me, she lingers on, saying good-bye again and again, fondling, kissing, admiring it, on her knees before me.

'A pure sweet virgin cunt! How long it is since I've seen one of those! To think—it has never been touched by man. That dear velvety maiden membrane—let me run my tongue once more across its delicious smooth surface—while it's still there! And those unfledged, unstretched lips, how nicely they kiss me back! And your lovely little joy-button, so small and sensitive and undeveloped. Oh, I must nibble it off!'

She suits the action to the word. It does not take a great deal of such delightful toying to reawaken my desires. My clitty stands up when spoken of with so much flattery. Nor does the gentle nibbling of her small regular teeth tend to lessen its self-consciousness. Little ripples of pleasure begin spreading from my cunny to my spine—But why worry the patient reader with a new recounting of what has just gone before? Only the delicious act itself bears repetition, and not with my inadequate words of attempted description. Suffice it to say that whether she had originally so intended or not, she accepts my gentle invitation to continue when I place my hands about the back of her pretty head and hold her more snugly to my reawakened cunt.

Scarcely a minute after she has begun, I come deliciously. But this climax I recognize as being just a part of my first thrill—a sort of warm wringing out of the remains of the earlier bacchanalia of pleasure—and so with continued importunities of my writhing hips, I wrap my thighs about her neck and shoulders and imprison her to a continuation of this delightful stimulation. Not at all unwilling, darling Nanette goes on, centering her dear labours of love exclusively upon my spongy little clitty for efficiency. I lie back on the bed and experience again her divine gamahuching. This time it takes a longer time for me to come—perhaps all of ten minutes—but, oh, dear reader, so delightful is the process of going to that 'come' that I am almost sorry when I arrive and it is all over. No—I lie. That third thrilling orgasm, though thinner, as it were, and less pervading (perhaps because of the familiarity with the paths over which the sensation has so recently blazed its way) was even sharper and more violently enjoyable than both those that went before. It left me sobbing and moaning in an overwhelming agony of bliss that—well, I am glad that I promised not to describe it, so completely would it defy my pen.

As I dressed, we exchanged our full names and became better acquainted in the more usual sense of the words. Also, we agreed to meet again in the early future.

Downstairs, I found that my marvellous adventure had occupied scarcely half-an-hour by the clock. Charley was sitting about disconsolately, consuming scores of cigarettes, alone except for a woman of the house who was wooing him in vain. All the other boys had retired with their respective choices and had not yet come down.

His eyes brightened when he spied me; but he was gloomy and sullen again when I sat down beside him.

'What kept you up there so long? A joke's a joke; but not when it's carried too far. One would think you were really up to something. What were you doing?'

'Oh—just chatting, to waste time. I didn't want to be the killjoy of the party and keep you from getting yourself a woman.'

'But don't you see, Louise?' he said earnestly, covering my hand with his and looking at me intensely with his handsome, pleading eyes, now seemingly shadowed by deep anguish, 'don't you see that I want no woman but you? I'm waiting for you. And damn it, I've been faithful to you for more than this half-hour that you've been gone.'

I blushed violently. My conscience was not clear.

'Charley,' I said, 'I'm afraid I'm scarcely worthy of this, your deep affection and unshaken faithfulness.'

He must have thought that he detected a note of sarcasm in my words, for he said roughly:

'Never mind, baby. I'm waiting.'

Randiana

I found at the age of thirty that I was only on the threshold of mysteries far more entrancing. I had up to that time been a mere man of pleasure, whose ample fortune (for my father, who had grown rich, did not disinherit me when he died) sufficed to procure any of those amorous delights without which the world would be a blank to me.

But further than the ordinary pleasures of the bed I had not penetrated.

'The moment was, however, approaching when all these would sink into significance before those greater sensual joys which wholesome and well applied flagellation will always confer upon its devotees.'

I quote the last sentence from a well-known author, but I'm far from agreeing with it in theory or principle.

I was emerging one summer's evening from the Café Royal, in Regent Street, with De Vaux, a friend of long standing, when he nodded to a gentleman passing in a 'hansom' who at once stopped the cab and got out.

'Who is it?' I said, for I felt a sudden and inexplicable interest in his large lustrous eyes, eyes such as I have never before seen in any human being.

'That is Father Peter, of St Martha of the Angels. He is a bircher, my boy, and one of the best in London.'

At this moment we were joined by the Father and a formal introduction took place.

I had frequently seen admirable *cartes* of Father Peter, or rather, as he preferred to be called, Monsignor Peter, in the shop windows of the leading photographers, and at once accused myself of being a doll not to have recognized him at first sight.

Descriptions are wearisome at the best, yet were I a clever novelist given to the art, I think I might even interest those of the sterner sex in Monsignor Peter, but although in the following paragraph I faithfully delineate him, I humbly ask his pardon if he should perchance in the years to come glance over these pages and think I have not painted his portrait in colours sufficiently glowing, for I must assure my readers that Father Peter is no imaginary Apollo, but one who in the present year of grace, 1883, lives, moves, eats, drinks, fucks, and flagellates with all the *verve* and dash he possessed at the date I met him first, now twenty-five years ago.

Slightly above the middle height and about my own age, or possibly a year my senior, with finely chiselled features and exquisite profile, Father Peter was what the world would term an exceedingly handsome man. It is true that perfectionists have pronounced the mouth a trifle too sensual and the cheeks a thought too plump for a standard of perfection, but the women would have deemed otherwise for the grand dreamy Oriental eyes, which would have outrivalled those of Byron's Gazelle, made up for any shortcoming.

The tonsure had been sparing in its dealings with his hair, which hung in thick but well-trimmed masses round a classic head, and as the slight summer breeze blew aside one lap of his long clerical coat, I noticed the elegant shape of his cods which, in spite of the tailor's art, would display their proportions to the evident admiration of one or two ladies who, pretending to look in at the windows of a draper near which we were standing seemed riveted to the spot, as the zephyrs revealed the tantalizing picture.

'I am pleased to make your acquaintance, Mr Clinton,' said Father Peter, shaking me cordially by the hand. 'Any friend of Mr De Vaux is a friend of mine. May I ask if either of you have dined yet?'

We replied in the negative.

'Then in that case, unless you have something better to do, I shall be glad if you will join me at my own home. I dine at seven, and am already rather late. I feel half-famished and was proceeding to Kensington, where my humble quarters are, when the sight of De Vaux compelled me to discharge the cab. What say you?'

'With all my heart,' replied De Vaux, and since I knew him to be a perfect sybarite at the table, and that his answer was based on a knowledge of Monsignor's resources, I readily followed suit.

To hail a four-wheeler and get to the doors of Father Peter's handsome but somewhat secluded dwelling, which was not very far from the south end of the long walk in Kensington Gardens, did not occupy more than twenty minutes.

Before many minutes he rejoined us, and leading the way, we followed him into one of the most lovely bijou *salons* it had ever been my lot to enter. There were seats for eight at the table, four of which were occupied, and the *chef* not waiting for his lord and master, had already sent up the soup.

I was briefly introduced, and De Vaux, who knew them all, had shaken himself into his seat before I found time to properly note the appearance of my neighbours.

Immediately on my left sat a complete counterpart of Monsignor himself, save that he was a much older man; his name, as casually mentioned to me, was Father Boniface, and although sparer in his proportions than Father Peter, his proclivities as a trencher-man belied his meagreness. He never missed a single course, and when anything particular tickled his gustatory sense, he had two or even more helpings.

Next to him sat a little short apoplectic man, a Doctor of Medicine, who was more of an epicure.

A sylph-like girl of sixteen occupied the next seat. Her fair hair, rather flaxen than golden-hued, hung in profusion down her back, while black lashes gave her violet eyes that shade which Greuze, the finest eye painter the world has ever seen, wept to think he could never exactly reproduce. I was charmed with her ladylike manner, her neatness of dress, virgin white, and above all, with the modest and unpretending way she replied to the questions put to her.

If ever there was a maid at sixteen under the blue vault of heaven, she sits there, was my involuntary thought, to which I nearly gave verbal expression, but was fortunately saved from such a frightful lapse by the page who, placing some appetizing salmon and lobster sauce before me, dispelled for the nonce my half visionary condition.

Monsignor P. sat near this young divinity, and ever and anon between the courses passed his soft white hands through her wavy hair.

I must admit I didn't half like it, and began to feel a jealous pang, but the knowledge that it was only the caressing hand of a Father of the Romish Church quieted me.

I was rapidly getting maudlin, and as I ate my salmon the smell of the lobster sauce suggested other thoughts till I found the tablecloth gradually rising, and I was obliged to drop my napkin on the floor to give myself the opportunity of adjusting my prick so that it would not be observed by the company.

I have omitted to mention the charmer who was placed between De Vaux and Father Peter. She was a lady of far maturer years than the sylph, and might be, as near as one could judge in the pale incandescent light which the pure filtered gas shed round with voluptuous radiance, about twenty-seven. She was a strange contrast to Lucy, for so my sylph was called. Tall, and with a singularly clear complexion for a brunette, her bust was beautifully rounded with that fullness of contour which, just avoiding the gross, charms without disgusting. Madeline, in short was in every inch a woman to chain a lover to her side.

I had patrolled the Continent in search of goods; I had overhauled every shape and make of cunt between Constantinople and Calcutta; but as I caught the liquid expressions of Madeline's large sensuous eyes, I confessed myself a fool.

Here in Kensington, right under a London clubman's nose was the *beau idéal* I had vainly travelled ten thousand miles to find. She was sprightliness itself in conversation, and I could not sufficiently thank De Vaux for having introduced me into such an Eden.

Lamb cutlets and cucumbers once more broke in upon my dream, and I was not at all sorry, for I found the violence of my thought had burst one of the buttons of my fly, a mishap I knew from past experience would be followed by the collapse of the others unless I turned my erratic brain wanderings into another channel, so that I kept my eyes fixed on my plate, absolutely afraid to gaze upon these two constellations again.

'As I observed just now,' said the somewhat fussy little Doctor, 'cucumber or cowcumber, it matters not much which, if philologists differ in the pronunciation surely we may.'

'The pronunciation,' said Father Peter, with a naive look at Madeline, 'is very immaterial, provided one does not eat too much of them. They are a dangerous plant, sir, they heat the blood, and we poor church-men, who have to chastize the lusts of the flesh, should avoid them *in toto*; yet I would fain have some more.' And suiting the actions to the word, he helped himself to a large quantity.

I should mention that I was sitting nearly opposite Lucy, and seeing her titter at the paradoxical method the worthy Father had of assisting himself to cucumber against his own argument, I thought it a favourable opportunity to show her that I sympa-thized with her mirth, so, stretching out my foot, I gently pressed her toe, and to my unspeakable joy she did not take her foot away, but rather, indeed, pushed it further in my direction.

I then, on the pretence of adjusting my chair, brought it a little nearer the table, and was in ecstasies when I perceived that Lucy not only guessed what my manoeuvres meant, but actually in a very sly puss-like way brought her chair nearer too.

Then balancing my arse on the edge of my seat as far as I could without being noticed, with my prick only covered with the table napkin, for it had with one wild bound burst all the remaining buttons on my breeches, I reached forward my foot, from which I had slid off my boot with the other toe, and in less than a minute I had worked it up so that I could just feel the heat of her fanny.

I will say this for her, she tried all she could to help me, but her cursed drawers were an insuperable obstacle, and I was foiled. I knew if I proceeded another inch I should inevitably come a cropper, and this knowledge, coupled with the fact that Lucy was turning wild with excitement, now red, now white, warned me to desist for the time being.

I now foresaw a rich conquest—something worth waiting for—and my blood coursed through my veins at the thought of the sweet little bower nestling within those throbbing thighs, for I could tell from the way her whole frame trembled how thoroughly mad she was at the trammels which society imposed. Not only that, the moisture on my stocking told me that it was something more than the dampness of perspiration, and I felt half sorry to think that I had 'jewgaged' her. At the same time, to parody the words of the poet laureate—

> *Tis better frigging with one's toe,*
> *Than never to have frigged at all.*

Some braised ham and roast fowls now came on, and I was astonished to find a poor priest of the Church of Rome launching out in this fashion. The Sauterne with the salmon had been simply excellent, and the Mumms, clear and sparkling, which accompanied the latter courses had fairly electrified me.

By the way, as this little dinner party may serve as

a lesson to some of those whose experience is limited, I will mention one strange circumstance which may account for much of what is to come.

Monsignor, when the champagne had been poured out for the first time, before any one had tasted it, went to a little liqueur stand, and taking from it a bottle of a most peculiar shape, added to each glass a few drops of the cordial.

'That is Pinero Balsam,' he said to me, 'you and one of the ladies have not dined at my table before, and, therefore, you may possibly never have tasted it, as it is but little known in England. It is compounded by one Italian firm only, whose ancestors, the Sagas of Venice, were the holders of the original recipe. Its properties are wondrous and manifold, but amongst others it rejuvenates senility, and those among us who have travelled *up and down* in the world a good deal and found the motion rather tiring as the years go on, have cause to bless its recuperative qualities.'

The cunning cleric by the inflection of his voice had sufficiently indicated his meaning and although the cordial was, so far as interfering with the champagne went, apparently tasteless, its effect upon the company soon began to be noticeable.

A course of ducklings, removed by Nesselrode pudding and Noyeau jelly, ended the repast, and after one of the shortest graces in Latin I had ever heard in my life, the ladies curtsied themselves out of the apartment, and soon the strains of a piano indicted that they had reached the drawing room, while we rose from the table to give the domestics an opportunity for clearing away.

My trousers were my chief thought at this moment, but I skilfully concealed the evidence of my passion with a careless pocket handkerchief, and my boot I accounted for by a casual reference to a corn of long standing.

'Gentlemen,' said Monsignor, lighting an exquisitely aromatized cigarette, for all priests, through the constant use of the senser, like the perfume of spices, 'first of all permit me to hope that you have enjoyed your dinner, and now I presume, De Vaux, your friend will not be shocked if we initiate him into the mysteries with which we solace the few hours of relaxation our priestly employment permits us to enjoy. Eh, Boniface?'

The latter, who was coarser than his superior, laughed boisterously.

'I expect, Monsignor, that Mr Clinton knows just as much about birching as we do ourselves.'

'I know absolutely nothing of it,' I said, 'and must even plead ignorance of the merest rudiments.'

'Well, sir,' said Monsignor, leaning back in his chair, 'the art of birching is one on which I pride myself that I can speak with greater authority than any man in Europe, and you may judge that I do not aver this from any self-conceit when I tell you that I have, during the last ten years, assisted by a handsome subsidy from the Holy Consistory at Rome, ransacked the known world for evidence in support of its history. In that escritoire,' he said, 'there are sixteen octavo volumes, the compilation of laborious research, in which I have been assisted by brethren of all the holy orders affiliated to Mother Church, and I may mention in passing that worthy Dr Prince here, and Father Boniface have both contributed largely from their wide store of experience in correcting and annotating many of the chapters which deal with recent discoveries, for, Mr Clinton, flagellation as an art is not only daily gaining fresh pupils and adherents, but scarcely a month passes without some new feature being added to our already huge stock of information.'

To tell the truth I scarcely appreciated all this, and felt a good deal more inclined to get upstairs to the drawing room, when just at this moment an incident occurred which gave me my opportunity.

The bonny brunette, Madeline, looked in at the door furtively and apologized, but reminded Monsignor that he was already late for vespers.

'My dear girl,' said the cleric, 'run over to the sacristy, and ask Brother Michael to officiate in my absence—the usual headache—and don't stay quite so long as you generally do, and if you should come back with your hair dishevelled and your dress in disorder, make up a better tale than you did last time.'

Or else your own may smart, I thought, for at this moment Father Boniface came in to ask Monsignor for another key to get the rods, as it appeared he had given him the wrong one.

Now is my time, I reflected, so making somewhat ostentatious inquiries as to the exact whereabouts of the lavatory, I quitted the apartment, promising to return in a few minutes.

I should not omit to mention that from the moment I drank the sparkling cordial that Father Peter had mixed with the champagne, my spirits had received an unwonted exhilaration, which I could not ascribe to natural causes.

I will not go so far as to assert that the augmentation of force which I found my prick to possess was entirely due to the Pinero Balsam, but this I will confidently maintain against all comers, that never had I felt so equal to any amorous exploit. It may have been the effect of a generous repast, it might have been the result of the toe-frigging I had indulged in; but as I stepped into the brilliantly lighted hall, and hastily passed upstairs to the luxurious drawing room, I could not help congratulating myself on the stubborn bar of iron which my unfortunately dismantled trousers could scarcely keep from popping out.

Fearing to frighten Lucy if I entered suddenly in a state of *déshabillé*, and feeling certain that a prick exhibition might tend to shock her inexperienced eye, I readjusted my bollocks, and peeped through the crack of the drawing-room door, which had been left temptingly half open.

There was Lucy reclining on the sofa in that *dolce far niente* condition which is a sure sign that a good dinner has agreed with one, and that digestion is waiting upon appetite like an agreeable and good-tempered handmaid should.

She looked so arch, and with such a charming pout upon her lips, that I stood there watching, half disinclined to disturb her dream.

It may be, I thought, that she is given to frigging herself, and being all alone she might possibly—but I speedily banished that thought, for Lucy's clear complexion and vigorous blue eyes forbade the suggestion.

At this instant something occurred which for the moment again led me to think that my frigging conjecture was about to be realized, for she reached her hand deliberately under her skirt, and lifting up her petticoats, dragged down the full length of her chemise, which she closely examined.

I divined it all at a glance: when I toe-frigged her in the dining room she had spent a trifle, and being her first experience of the kind, could not understand.

So she really is a maid after all, I thought, and as I saw a pair of shapely lady-like calves encased in lovely pearl silk stockings of a light blue colour, I could retain myself no longer, and with a couple of bounds was at her side before she could recover herself.

'Oh! Mr Clinton. Oh! Mr Clinton; how could you,' was all she found breath or thought to ejaculate.

I simply threw my arms around her and kissed her flushed face, *on the cheeks*, for I feared to frighten her too much at first.

At last, finding she lay prone and yielding, I imprinted a kiss upon her mouth, and found it returned with ardour.

Allowing my tongue to gently insinuate itself into her half-open mouth and touch hers, I immediately discovered that her excitement, as I fully expected, became doubled, and without saying a word I guided her disengaged hand to my prick, which she clutched with the tenacity of a drowning man catching at a floating spar.

'My own darling,' I said, and waiting for no further encouragement, I pushed my right hand softly up between her thighs, which mechanically opened to give it passage.

To say that I was in the seventh heaven of delight, as my warm fingers found a firm plump cunt with a rosebud hymen as yet unbroken, is but faintly to picture my ecstasy.

To pull her a little way further down on the couch so that her rounded arse would rise in the middle and make the business a more convenient one, was the work of a second; the next I had withdrawn my prick from her grasp and placed it against the lips of her quim, at the same time easing them back with a quick movement of my thumb and forefinger. I gave one desperate lunge, which made Lucy cry out 'Oh God,' and the joyful deed was consummated.

As I have hinted before, my prick was no joke in the matter of size, and upon this occasion, so intense was the excitement that had led up to the fray, it was rather bigger than usual; but thanks to the heat the sweet virgin was in, the sperm particles of her vagina were already resolved into grease, which, mixing with the few drops of blood caused by the violent separation of the hymeneal cord, resulted in making the friction natural and painless. Not only that, once inside I found Lucy's fanny was internally framed on a very free-and-easy scale, and here permit me to digress and point out the ways of Nature.

Some women She frames with an orifice like an exaggerated horse collar, but with a passage more fitted for a tin whistle than a man's prick, while in others the opening itself is like the tiniest wedding ring, though if you once get inside your prick is in the same condition as the poor devil who floundered up the biggest cunt on record and found another bugger looking for his hat. Others again—but why should I go on in this prosy fashion, when Lucy has only received half-a-dozen strokes, and is on the point of coming?

What a delicious process we went through; even to recall it after all these years, now that Lucy is a staid matron, the wife of a church rector, and the mother of two youths verging on manhood, is bliss, and will in my most depressed moments always suffice to give me a certain and prolonged erection.

The beseeching blue eyes that glanced up at Monsignor's drawing-room ceiling, as though in silent adoration and heartfelt praise at the warm stream I seemed to be spurting into her very vitals. The quick nervous shifting of her fleshy buttocks, as she strove to ease herself of her own pent-up store of liquid; and then the heartfelt sigh of joy and relief that escaped her ruby lips as I withdrew my tongue and she discharged the *sang de la vie* at the same moment.

Oh! there is no language copious enough to do justice to the acme of a first fuck, nor is there under God's sun a nation which has yet invented a term sufficiently comprehensive to picture the emotions of a man's mind as he mounts a girl he knows from digital proof to be a maid as pure in person, and as innocent of prick, dildo, or candle as arctic snow.

Scarcely had I dismounted and reassured Lucy with a serious kiss that it was all right, and that she need not alarm herself, when Madeline came running in.

'Oh! Lucy,' she cried, 'such fun—' Then, seeing me, she abruptly broke off with—'I beg your pardon, Mr Clinton, I did not see you were here.'

Lucy, who was now in a sitting posture, joined in the conversation, and I saw by the ease of her manner that she had entirely recovered her self-possession, and that I could rejoin the gentlemen downstairs.

'Do tell those stupid men not to stay there over their cigars all day. It is paying us no compliment,' was Madeline's parting shot.

In another moment I was in my seat again, and prepared for a resumption of Monsignor's lecture on birch rods.

'Where the Devil have you been to, Clinton?' said De Vaux.

'Where it would have been quite impossible for you to have acted as my substitute,' I unhesitatingly replied.

My answer made them all laugh, for they thought I referred to the water closet, whereas I was of course alluding to Lucy, and I knew I was stating a truism in that case as regarded De Vaux, for he was scarcely yet convalescent from a bad attack of Spanish glanders, which was always his happy method of expressing the clap.

'Now my dear Mr Clinton, I wish you particularly to observe the tough fibre of these rods,' said Monsignor Peter, as he handed me a bundle so perfectly and symmetrically arranged that I could not help remarking on it.

'Ah!' exclaimed Monsignor, 'that is a further proof of how popular the flagellating art has become. So large a trade is being done, sir, in specially picked birch of the flagellating kind, that they are hand-sorted by children and put up in bundles by machinery, as they appear here, and my own impresson is that if the Canadian Government were to impose an extra duty on these articles, for they almost come under the heading of manufactures and not produce, a large revenue would accrue; but enough of this,' said the reverend gentleman, seeing his audience was becoming somewhat impatient. 'You saw at the dinner table the young lady I addressed as Lucy.'

I reflected for a moment to throw them off their guard, and then said, suddenly, 'Oh, yes, the sweet thing in white.'

'Well,' continued Monsignor Peter, 'her father is a long time dead, and her mother is in very straitened circumstances; the young girl herself is a virgin, and I have this morning paid to her mother a hundred pounds to allow her to remain in my house for a month or so with the object of initiating her.'

'Initiating her into the Church?' I inquired, laughing to myself, for I knew that her initiation in other respects was fairly well accomplished.

'No,' smiled Monsignor, touching the rods significantly, 'this is the initiation to which I refer.'

'What,' I cried, aghast, 'are you going to birch her?'

'We are,' put in Dr Price. 'Her first flagellation will be tonight, but this is merely an experimental one. A few strokes well administered, and a quick fuck after to determine my work on corpuscular action of the blood particles; tomorrow she will be in better form to receive second class instruction, and we hope by the end of the month—'

'To have a perfect pupil,' put in Father, who did not relish Dr Price taking the lead on a flagellation subject, 'but let us proceed to the drawing room. Boniface, put that bundle in the birch box and bring it upstairs.'

So saying, the chief exponent of flagellation in the known world led the way upstairs to the drawing room, and we followed, though I must confess that in my case it was with no slight trepidation, for I felt somehow as though I were about to assist at a sacrifice.

As we entered the room we found Lucy in tears, and Madeline consoling her, but she no sooner saw us than, breaking from her friend, she threw herself at Monsignor's feet, and clinging to his knees, sobbed out—

'Oh, Father Peter, you have always been a kind friend to my mother and myself, do say that the odious tale of shame that girl has poured into my ears is not true.'

'Good God!' I muttered, 'they have actually chosen Madeline as the instrument to explain what they are about to do.'

'Rise, my child,' said Monsignor, 'do not distress yourself but listen to me.' Half bearing the form of the really terrified young thing to the couch, we gathered round in a circle and listened.

'You doubtless know, my sweet daughter,' began the wily and accomplished priest, 'that the votaries of science spare neither friends nor selves in their efforts to unravel the secrets of nature. Time and pain are no object to them, so that the end be accomplished.'

To this ominous introduction Lucy made no response.

'You have read much, daughter of mine,' said Monsignor, stroking her silken hair, 'and when I tell you that your dead father devoted you to the fold of Mother Church, and that your mother and I both think you will best be serving Her ends and purposes by submitting yourself to those tests which will be skilfully carried out without pain, but on the contrary, with an amount of pleasure such as you cannot even guess at, you will probably acquiesce.'

Lucy's eyes here caught mine, and although I strove to reassure her with a look that plainly intimated no harm should come to her, she was some time before she at last put her hand in the cleric's and said—

'Holy Father, I do not think you would allow

anything very dreadful; I will submit, for my mother, when I left her this morning, told me above all else to be obedient to you in everything and trust you implicitly.'

'That is my own trump of a girl,' said Monsignor, surprised for the first time during the entire evening into a slang expression, but I saw his large round orbs gloating over his victim, and his whole frame trembled with excitement as he led Lucy into the adjoining apartment and left her alone with Madeline.

'Now, gentlemen,' said Monsignor, 'the moment approaches, and you will forgive me, Mr Clinton, if I have to indulge in a slight coarseness of language, but time presses and plain Saxon is the quickest method of expression. Personally, I do not feel inclined to fuck Lucy myself, as a matter of fact I had connection with her mother the night previous to her marriage, and as Lucy was born exactly nine months afterwards, I am rather in doubt as to the paternity.

In other words,' I said, astounded, 'you think it possible that you may be her father.'

'Precisely,' said Monsignor. 'You see that the instant the flagellation is ended, somebody must necessarily fuck her, and personally my objection prevents me. Boniface here, prefers boys to women, and Dr Price will be too busy taking notes, so that it rests between you and De Vaux, who had better toss up.'

De Vaux, who was stark mad to think that his little gonorrheal disturbance was an insuperable obstacle, pleaded an engagement later on, which he was bound to fulfil, and therefore, Monsignor Peter told me to be sure to be ready the instant I was wanted.

Madeline entered at this moment and informed us

that all was ready, but gave us to understand that she had experienced the greatest difficulty in overcoming poor Lucy's natural scruples at being exposed in all her virgin nakedness to the gaze of so many of the male sex.

'She made a very strange observation, too,' continued Madeline, looking at me with a drollery I could not understand, 'she said, "if it had been only Mr Clinton, I don't think I should have minded quite so much." '

'Oh! all the better,' said Father Peter, 'for it is Mr Clinton who will have to relieve her at the finish.'

With these words we proceeded to the birching room, which it appears had been furnished by these professors of flagellation with a nicety of detail, and an eye to everything accessory to the art that was calculated to inspire a neophyte like myself with the utmost astonishment.

On a framework of green velvet was a soft down bed, and reclined on this length was the blushing Lucy.

Large bands of velvet, securely buckled at the sides, held her in position, while her legs, brought well together and fastened in the same way, slightly elevated her soft shapely arse.

The elevation was further aided by an extra cushion, which had been judiciously placed under the lower portion of her belly.

Monsignor bent over her and whispered a few soothing words into her ear, but she only buried her delicate head deeper into the down of the bed, while the reverend Father proceeded to analyse the points of her arse.

Having all of them felt her arse in turn, pinching

it as though to test its condition, much as a connoisseur in horseflesh would walk around an animal he was about to buy, Monsignor at length said—

'What a superb picture.' His eyes were nearly bursting from their sockets. 'You must really excuse me, gentlemen, but my feelings overcome me,' and taking his comely prick out of his breeches, he deliberately walked up to Madeline, and before that fair damsel had guessed his intentions, he had thrown her down on the companion couch to Lucy's and had fucked her heart out in a shorter space of time than it takes me to write it.

To witness this was unutterably maddening. I scarcely knew what to be at, my heart beat wildly, and I should then and there have put it into Lucy myself had I not been restrained by Father Boniface who, arch-vagabond that he was, took the whole business as a matter of course and merely observed to Monsignor that it would be as well to get it over as soon as possible, since Mr Clinton was in a devil of a hurry.

Poor Lucy was deriving some consolation from Dr Price in the shape of a few drops of Pinero Balsam in champagne, while as for De Vaux, he was groaning audibly, and when the worthy Father Peter came to the short strokes De Vaux's chordee became so unbearable that he ran violently out into Monsignor's bedroom, as he afterwards informed me, to bathe his balls in ice water.

To me there was something rather low and shocking in a fuck before witnesses, but that is a squeamishness that I have long since got the better of.

Madeline, having wiped Monsignor's prick with a

piece of *mousseline de laine*, a secret known only to the sybarite in love's perfect secrets, retired, presumably to syringe her fanny, and Monsignor buttoned up and approached his self-imposed task.

Taking off his coat he turned up his short cuffs and, Boniface handing him the birch rods, the bum-warming began.

At the first keen swish poor Lucy shrieked out, but before half a dozen had descended with a quick smacking sound which betokens that there is no lack of elbow grease in the application, her groans subsided, and she spoke in a quick strained voice, begging for mercy.

'For the love of God,' she said, 'do not, pray do not lay it on so strong.'

By this time her lovely arse had assumed a flushed, vermilion tinge, which appeared to darken with every stroke, and at this point Dr Price interposed.

'Enough, Monsignor, now my duty begins.' And quick as thought he placed upon her bottom a piece of linen, which was smeared with an unguent, and struck it at the sides with a small modicum of tar plaster to prevent it from coming off.

'Oh!' cried Lucy, 'I feel so funny. Oh! Mr Clinton, if you are there, pray relieve me, and make haste.'

In an instant my trousers were down, the straps were unbuckled, and Lucy was gently turned over on her back.

I saw a delicate bush of curly hair, a pair of glorious thighs, and the sight impelled me to thrust my prick into that divine Eden I had visited but a short time before with an ardour that for a man who had lived a fairly knockabout life was inexplicable.

I had scarcely got it thoroughly planted, and had

certainly not made a dozen well-sustained though rapid strokes, before the gush of sperm which she emitted drew me at the same instant, and I must own that I actually thought the end of the world had come.

'Now,' said Dr Price, rapidly writing in his pocket-book, 'you see that my theory was correct. Here is a maid who has never known a man and she spends within ten seconds of the entrance being effected. Do you suppose that without the birching she could have performed such a miracle?'

'Yes,' I said, 'I do, and I can prove that all your surmises are but conjecture, and that even your conjecture is based upon a fallacy.'

'Bravo,' said Father Peter, 'I like to see Price fairly collared. Nothing flabbergasts him like facts. Dear me, how damnation slangy I am getting tonight. Lucy, dear, don't stand shivering there, slip on your things and join Madeline in my snuggery; we shall all be there presently. Go on, Clinton.'

'Well,' I said, 'it is easy enough to refute the learned Doctor. In the first place Lucy was not a maid.'

'That be damned for a tale,' said Father Boniface. 'I got her mother to let me examine her myself last night while she was asleep, previous to handing over the hundred pounds.'

'Yes, that I can verify,' said Monsignor, 'though I must admit that you have a prick like a kitchen poker, for you got into her as easy as though she'd been on a Regent Street round for twenty years.'

'I will bet anyone here 50 to 1,' I said, quietly taking out my pocketbook, 'that she was not a maid before I poked her just now.'

'Done,' said the Doctor who, upon receiving a knowing wink from Father Peter, felt sure he was going to bag two ponies, 'and now how are we to prove it?'

'Ah, that will be difficult,' said Monsignor.

'Not at all,' I observed, 'let the young lady be sent for and questioned on the spot where you assume she was first deflowered of her virginity.'

'Yes, that's fair,' said De Vaux, and accordingly he called her in.

'My dear Lucy,' said Monsignor, 'I wish you to tell me the truth in answer to a particular question I am about to put to you.'

'I certainly will,' said Lucy, 'for God knows I have literally nothing now to conceal from you.'

'Well, that's not bad for a *double entente*,' said the Father, laughing, 'but now tell us candidly, before Mr Clinton was intimate with you in our presence just now, had you ever before had a similar experience?'

'Once,' said Lucy, simpering, and examining the pattern of the carpet.

'Good God,' said the astonished Churchman, as with deathlike silence he waited for an answer to his next question.

'When was it and with whom?'

'With Mr Clinton himself, in the drawing room here, about an hour ago.'

I refused the money of course, but had the laugh on all of them, and as we rolled home to De Vaux's chambers in a hansom about an hour later I could not help admitting to him that I considered the evening we had passed through the most agreeable I had ever known.

'You will soon forget it in the midst of other pleasures.'

'Never,' I said. 'If Calais was graven on Mary's

heart I am quite sure that this date will be found inscribed on mine if ever they should hold an inquest upon my remains.'

The Loves of Lord
Roxboro

Preparing herself for the bath, Caroline heard the murmur of voices from the library next to her bedroom, so stepping to the door, she listened for a moment but could distinguish nothing but a mumble. Searching the door, she discovered a tiny crevice through which she could peep into the adjoining room. Applying her eyes to the opening, she looked into the library and saw her uncle seated in a chair, while standing before him, her hands clasped and a beseeching look in her eyes, stood Marie, the maid.

Caroline stood gazing through the crevice in the door and as she discovered who the occupants of the room were, she found she could faintly hear their conversation, although they were apparently talking in low voices.

'Marie,' said Lord Roxboro, 'you have been with me now for some time. You have served me well and I have no particular fault to find with you.'

'Yes, sir, thank you, sir,' said Marie looking at Roxboro wonderingly.

'I make it a point, Marie,' he continued, drawing a paper from his pocket, which he unfolded and glanced over, 'I make it a point to investigate all of my employees thoroughly. You have been with me now for three months, I believe?' he asked, raising his eyes to the pretty maid.

'Nearly four, sir,' she answered.

'Of small matter,' he remarked. 'You gave references when you came here of people that resided in your hometown, Middleboro, is it not?'

'Yes, sir, that is right,' answered Marie, looking a trifle worried at the trend the conversation was taking, and shifting her feet nervously.

'I find,' he continued, referring to the paper, 'I find that you are well known in Middleboro. In fact, to be quite frank with you, my dear, much too well known in certain quarters! Do you happen to know a certain Mr Montgomery, Marie?'

At the mention of this name, Marie blanched and seemed about to swoon. Her lips paled out, controlling herself with an effort, she stood with downcast eyes before her employer.

'I thought that name would touch home!' cried Lord Roxboro with a satisfied air. 'My suspicions, I see, are well grounded. You know him, do you?'

'Yes, sir,' answered Marie, her answer barely audible to Caroline as she listened at the peephole.

'And this man, this man Montgomery, was he your lawfully wedded husband? Is this right, Marie?'

'Yes, sir,' she answered again, clenching her hands until the knuckles whitened, twitching about as she tried to evade her employer's stern and inquiring glance.

'And you, the lawfully wedded spouse of this man Montgomery, ran away and deserted him? And when decamping, took all of his money and his watch and other valuables?' the lord shot at the shrinking girl.

'Oh, that is untrue, sir!' she replied with flashing eyes. 'He beat me and starved me and made me leave him! I never wanted to be his wife and the act of marriage was against my will. I was forced into a union with the detestable creature!'

Lord Roxboro cast a sensual glance mingled with pure admiration at the beautiful creature as she stood radiant in her youthful beauty, denying the aspersions cast upon her honesty.

'Easy now, Marie,' he soothed her. 'You left him, at least, and took with you when you left the money and the jewellery that I have just mentioned. Is that not right?'

'Yes, my lord,' she answered in a low tone.

'And you came into my employ and lied to me about these happenings, knowing very well that this husband of yours, this Mr Montgomery, had already filed charges with the authorities against you for theft and that at this very moment the authorities are in search of you? Have you been honest and fair with me, I ask you?'

'Oh, no, sir,' she sobbed. 'I could never bring myself to tell you of those dreadful happenings. Has he really filed charges against me, as you say, and are the police in search of me?' Here she clasped her tiny hands together and glanced beseechingly at his lordship.

'They are hunting for you at this very moment,' said Lord Roxboro sternly. 'And if I should perform my duty as a landowner, I would call them at once and allow them to convey you back to Middleboro, to jail, where you rightfully belong, you shameless creature!' At this his eyes glowed with righteous indignation.

'Oh, master!' cried Marie, throwing herself on her knees and clasping Lord Roxboro's hand as it lay on the arm of the chair, casting her beautiful eyes, now bedimmed with tears of crystal, upon him. 'Oh, master, I beg of you! Do not turn me off like this, do not give me up! Montgomery was a devil, indeed! I married him at seventeen, knowing nothing of the world or its evil devices! I have suffered for my sins, and I have been so happy during the short time I have worked for you and only want to stay here. Be fair with me, if this doesn't please you, and take into consideration the faithful services that I have rendered to you; and if you will not allow me to remain, at least allow me to depart from here in peace! Anywhere will I flee to escape the machinations of this dreadful nemesis, the man who was my husband! I have been a true servant and have tried to do my best. Forgive me if I lied to you before; what I saw now is the truth!'

'Yes, but you have lied to me once, Marie,' replied the lord. 'Who knows whether you are truthful with me now or not?' Upon her continued protestations that she was indeed telling the truth, he arose and paced the floor nervously.

'Then you don't deny that you stole the things mentioned, Marie?' he said, turning to her as she softly sobbed, her head buried in the chair. 'You stole them?'

'Yes, my lord,' she sobbed, 'I stole just enough to enable me to leave him. He would give me no money and I could not stand his brutal ways any longer. He whipped and beat me!'

'How old are you now, Marie?'

'Eighteen, last month,' she said, turning her tear-dimmed eyes upward to him as he questioned her.

'Go to my desk and procure me ink and paper,' he commanded. She scrambled to her feet, went to the desk and procured the articles, placing them upon the table before which he stood, then took her station a few feet away. The lord wrote rapidly for a moment or two, then, reading over what he had written and making a few changes, extended the pen to the maid.

'Marie, I have written an outline of the charges that have been preferred against you. They are here on this paper and I wish you to sign it. It is what you might term a sort of confession. Come, sign.'

'But, my lord,' she remonstrated, 'you aren't going to turn me over to the police, are you? You wouldn't make me go back to that beast, Montgomery, would you? Why are you asking me to sign that paper?'

'That remains to be seen, Marie,' he replied. 'You have confessed here to me, just a moment ago, that you are guilty of the crime charged against you. I really should have turned you over to the police at once. If you will kindly sign this document, I may give you another chance and allow you to continue here in my employ. Of course, you may use your own judgment. I can summon the police if you wish it,' and he turned to the bell cord as if to pull it.

'No, no, sir,' cried the panic-stricken Marie, seizing the pen and scribbling her name at the lower part of the document. 'I will do as you wish, my lord; you allow me another chance to prove my faithfulness. Oh, thank you so much. There you are, sir, I have signed it as you directed!' and throwing the pen on the table, she burst into a torrent of heartbreaking sobs.

Lord Roxboro made no answer, but picking up the paper, he again read it over carefully, and walking to the side of the room where the safe stood, he twirled the knob and opened the heavy door. Depositing the paper in one of the smaller drawers, he closed the door and twirled the knob. Caroline was a breathless spectator to all of this and stood with her eyes glued to the peephole, wondering what would happen next.

Lord Roxboro again seated himself in the armchair, placing his hand on top of Marie's head as she knelt sobbing upon the floor at his side, patting it for a moment, allowing his fingers to run through the fine tendrils of her dark hair and said in a gentle voice:

'Come, Marie, arise and seat yourself on the arm of this chair. I have several things I want to ask you about.'

The weeping girl arose from her kneeling posture on the floor, and following her employer's directions, seated herself alongside him upon the arm of the chair and with a tiny wisp of linen handkerchief attempted to dry her luminous eyes.

'To think that you, my little maid, Marie, were married!' said Lord Roxboro, grasping one of the girls's tiny hands in his own and softly patting it. 'Why, Marie, I thought that you knew little or nothing about such things. Were you with your husband any great length of time?'

'Nearly a year,' she answered, 'but it seemed a lifetime.'

'Don't think, Marie,' he continued, 'that because I do not turn you over to the police that you are entirely free. You have committed theft and you should be properly punished. You must either work out your salvation here with me, or in the workhouse. I assure you, my girl, that I have no present intention of letting you off scot-free. No, not in the least. You must understand that, don't you, Marie?'

'Yes, my lord,' she answered penitently. 'I am extremely grateful for your generosity in this matter, and assure you that you will have no reason to regret it. I will work for you as I have never worked before. I will do my best to please you. You certainly may depend upon it, my lord.'

'Work!' laughed Lord Roxboro. 'It is not a question of work, my dear girl. I desire you to clearly understand the situation. I have the power, if I wish to exercise it, whenever I desire it, to turn you over to the proper authorities. That little bit of paper that is securely held in that safe, attested with your name, is sufficient to convict you in any court in the land and to bring you a long term in the reformatory. Realize that part of it clearly, Marie! You and I must have no misunderstanding along that line. You are fully and completely in my power. Your punishment for this cold-blooded thievery must be fixed and regulated by myself, your master. Remember that!'

'Yes, my lord,' murmured the girl submissively. 'I understand the situation thoroughly, and whatever you decide will be all right, only please don't send me to jail and don't send me back to that brute, my husband! Anything, anything you say, I will be glad to do.'

'We will see later on,' he said, and throwing his arms about the neck of the lovely girl and drawing her face down to his, he presented an impassioned kiss upon the full red lips. She made no struggle to escape, but seemed to react to his impassioned caress, her soft bare arms stealing about his neck, holding him in a close embrace as he rained kisses upon her cherry lips.

Caroline was by now quite warmed by this tender scene. She saw Roxboro's hand steal to the front of Marie's waist, which he unbuttoned, drawing forth her well-shaped breasts, which he proceeded to fondle and squeeze and finally to kiss and gently bite, then allowing them to hang free in sensual looseness from her waist. Caroline envied the girl these soul-titillating touches, and at the sight of her passionate uncle fondling this beautiful maiden, strange feelings coursed through her body.

'Go lock the door, Marie,' commanded the lord, rising to his feet and gently pushing the now flushed girl toward the entrance to the library.

Marie, her breasts still hanging freely from her opened waist, ran to the door and pushed home the bolt. Returning to his lordship, who had by now seated himself upon a couch, she sat beside him, this move bringing both persons directly opposite to the peeping Caroline's line of vision, and when Lord Roxboro again clasped the palpitating girl to him, she responded to his warm kisses.

Caroline, a close spectator of these toyings of love, saw her uncle's inquiring hand creep up under Marie's skirts. The impassioned girl allowed herself to sink back on the couch, her legs slowly spreading as though to permit her sensual employer to ply his exploring fingers without hindrance.

At this movement, the sensual lord dragged up her skirts to the waistline, and the watching Caroline was rewarded with a full unobstructed view of the beautiful maid's lower person.

Her entire lower body was uncovered, as she wore no drawers, with silken stockings of fine texture, which were held in place by a pair of beautiful pink silk garters, and as the inquiring fingers of the lord pulled apart the girl's willing thighs and one of them inserted itself into the dense hair that covered her lower belly with a soft silken growth, fingering the throbbing cove beneath. Caroline wiggled her buttocks with passion, at the same time her own finger stealing into that centre of femine bliss, which she titillated violently in sympathy with the erotic scene before her enchanted eyes.

Marie lay back, almost prone, her thighs outspread to her employer's busy fingers. Caroline caught a glimpse of the passion-swollen lips as her uncle slowly massaged the dewy interior. Finally, evidently deeming that this provocative handling might cause the beautiful girl a premature orgasm, he slowly withdrew his hand, and Caroline, the entire scene directly before her interested eyes, could hardly repress a cry of astonishment at the gaping cleft that was left exposed to her startled eyes.

What an opening this was! Surely her own was not so dilated as that of this beautiful girl! It beamed with a dewy moisture, and as the enraptured Caroline watched it, it seemed to pulse and leap, probably from the soul-stirring fingerings it had received from her uncle's busy digits.

At this moment Lord Roxboro quickly unfastened the fly of his pantaloons, and the delightful object of Caroline's admiration sprang forth, erect and hard, as though to do battle with the pulsating quim that was so near it. Marie, needing no coaching or instruction in the delectable art, immediately grasped the huge bolus in one of her tendril-like hands and slowly massaged and squeezed its gigantic length, her fingers running quickly from the flaming head to the heavy pendulous balls that depended from this gigantic stabber.

The titillations of the beautiful girl's fingers upon his manly rod seemed to have a thrilling effect upon

Lord Roxboro, and he wiggled and leaped at each compression and relaxation of her dainty fingers. Suddenly pushing the girl backward upon the couch, he sprang astride of her and Caroline saw him bury his flaming prong in Marie's throbbing cunt!

Each and every downward stroke and the accompanying sweet withdrawal was watched with eager eyes by the interested girl, whose eye was glued intently to the peephole; and as she watched the wiggling, twisting, sighing couple, each uttering sweet groans and sighs of pleasure, her busy finger frigged that centre of sensual pleasure on her own person in sympathy with the couple so busy in love's action on the couch before her.

Presently, with a few short, frantic plunges that almost seemed to drive his banger home and that seemed to paralyze the wiggling girl beneath him, Lord Roxboro reached the quintessence of bliss and poured forth into the lascivious maid a full stream of love's elixir; the girl at the same time reached her climax, and with a few short, spasmodic plunges and writhings, the two sank exhausted upon the couch, panting from their exertions.

At the same time, Caroline, seeing that the two were approaching the desired moment, had worked herself into a frenzy with her fingers, and when they reached the apogee of bliss, she accompanied them with a self-induced orgasm that nearly caused her to faint with passion and pleasure.

Lord Roxboro, after lying a moment in that sweet, soothing after-ecstasy, upon the body of the beautiful girl who still sighed softly beneath him, her cleft distended by his throbbing tool, arose staggering to his feet, his noble rod drooping and soft, sticky with their combined dew, and, walking to the bathroom, secured a towel and dried his parts.

Truly, this amorous sport must be extremely exhilarating to some members of the feminine sex. Caroline had never seen the maid look so radiant as now she did.

For a moment Caroline supposed that the episode was finished, in her ignorance little suspecting the calibre of the two persons engaged in this battle of love. She kept watch, however, with the idea of missing nothing that might transpire further, and her vigil was duly rewarded.

After Lord Roxboro had cleansed his parts with the towel, Marie laughingly reached for the cloth. Throwing her dresses high, allowing her parts to become thoroughly visible to the watching Caroline and his sensual lordship, she thrust the towel between her legs and dried herself, vigorously rubbing the towel against her sensitive parts with a grimace of passion as the rough texture of the cloth touched the still tingling centres of sensation. This act finished, she permitted her dress to fall and once more seated herself upon the edge of the couch. Lord Roxboro, buttoning his pantaloons, seated himself beside her, and gathering the charming maid into his arms, smothered her with hot kisses.

'You have been pretty well opened up by your husband.' The girl laughed at this and glued her willing lips to his for a lingering embrace. It seemed that she was in that parched condition so well known to widows, and the recent happenings had only increased her passionate desire.

'You are quite a kisser too, my dear,' said the

recipient of the girl's warm embraces. 'Your devoted husband must have taught you that lingering, soul-searing French kiss that you perform so expertly. What a pretty tongue you have, my dear Marie! Thrust it forth for my inspection and allow me to look at that titillating member that has wrought such sad havoc with my manly feelings.'

The girl thrust out her pink tongue and sensuously wiggled its strawberry tip, darting it to and fro, in and out of her pretty mouth for the lord's inspection. Fired by this lascivious exhibition, he sought to embrace the beautiful girl once more, but she laughingly dodged her head from beneath his encircling arm and bent it forward to the man's lap, holding him tightly about the waist with both arms.

'Aha!' cried the lord. 'I am of the opinion that you are quite accomplished in certain ways and devices of exciting the passions. I feel certain that you are well versed in quite a number of practices that I did not, in my blindness, credit you with, you little teaser!' Patting the back of her head with his hand and running his fingers through her hair and about her shell-like ears, he massaged the back of her neck and head, which she had buried in the front of his lap.

'We will soon see how much you know, my little Venus!' cried her uncle. The breathless Caroline from her vantage point watched interestedly as her uncle leaned back and unbuttoned the front of his shirt, baring his manly breast, covered with hair, the brown nipples of his breast standing forth; then, lifting the fair girl's head, he pressed it against his breast and held her closely to him.

Caroline, profiting by the knowledge imparted to her by her sensual uncle, together with womanly intuition, realized that the beautiful maid was busily engaged in tonguing her uncle's nipples. His hand was busy at the buttons on his trousers, then suddenly the head of his member leaped forth, about half-hard but becoming rampant under the ministrations of the lovely girl.

The man's whole front body was now exposed, and the salacious girl, busy with her adroit tongue, slipped down his bare belly, weaving from side to side in her lascivious downward course, missing not a spot on his entire front, until, slipping to her knees on the floor directly in front of the impassioned lord, she tongued up and down his groin, causing her master to writhe in passion.

In another moment the watching Caroline saw the kneeling maid, apparently flaming with lust, suddenly engulf the man's rod in her rosy lips. Sucking it violently for a moment, she released it and her busy tongue licked its sides and head, thence downward toward the hairy sack which she titillated with her dartlike tongue. Then working back upward again, her tongue slid up and down the now throbbing shaft of the man's resurrected tool; reaching the head, she once more plunged it into her mouth until Caroline wondered how Marie could accommodate the huge member without choking upon it.

The lord's hands slipped down about the fair operator's neck, hugging her head close to his belly, and thrust forth his lower parts to meet the action of the girl's head as it worked up and down upon the shaft of his huge prick.

His hands now worked downward and grasped the girl's beautiful bare bubbies, which he massaged and crushed as the maid sucked and chewed upon his swollen member. This lively encounter raged for a few moments, the girl at times being forced to pause for breath, only to engulf once more that now iron-hard instrument within her distended jaws and move gently yet rapidly up and down upon it with a slight swinging motion.

Under the eager gaze of the interested spectator, the pace livened a bit; Lord Roxboro's grip on the neck of the fair manipulator tightened as though he would crush it between his hands, and he now moved his buttocks with frantic emotion. Caroline saw her uncle's staff leap and plunge as he endeavoured to plunge it to the hilt within the fair one's mouth, she only saving herself from being choked by the massive charger by grasping it firmly at the root with one tightly encircling hand; the lord's face contorted with passion and his eyes closed as the girl now sucked on that fleshy morsel with furious intensity, and as his staff throbbed and panted, Caroline knew that her uncle was now pumping into the eager and willing throat of the pretty maid the very essence of his being!

The lord, trembling as if in an ague, held the fair girl tightly to him as she mouthed and sucked, the convulsions of the muslces of her neck telling of the balsamic cargo that was now oiling her throat; and she choked, grasped, and strangled until the man's sensual grasp finally loosened about her neck and she fell, a sodden, panting heap, upon the carpet, and the lord slumped back upon the couch, thoroughly overcome by his recent passion and exertions!

My Secret Life

In the year 18** I walked up P***l**d P***e at about
ten o'clock at night, and saw a tall woman standing
at the corner of L**t*e P***l**d Street. Her size
attracted me, I spoke, and offering half a sovereign
with the understanding that she would take everything off—went with her to a house in L**t*e P***
l**d Street.

She kept her word and stripped whilst I sat looking
on.—When in her chemise,—Do you want me quite
naked?'—'Yes.' Then she slipped it off and stood stark
naked, boots, stockings, and garters, excepted.—I
may as well describe her at once, as for quite four
years, she satisfied almost every sexual want, and
helped me to satisfy every sensual fantasy.

She was with the exception of the second Camille
(the French woman) almost the most quiet, regular,
complacent woman I had had since that time, and
moreoever was most serviceable to me in all my pleasures, ministering to them as I wanted them—but
rarely herself suggesting them.—Ready to undertake
anything for me, and after some length of intimacy
participating in, and well pleased with, our erotic
amusements; never attempting to exact money, but
always content, and at length getting so accustomed
to me that she let me into much knowledge of her
private daily life.

She was I should say five feet nine or nearly ten
high, which is tall for a woman. Her hips were when
viewed from the front, of the proper width for such a

234

height—but her shoulders somewhat narrow. Altho so tall, she was small boned and plump all over, yet she had not an atom of what may be called fatness; had a small foot, a fine shaped calve, and thighs not quite so large proportionately. Her bum with fine firm round cheeks was not heavy at the back, was rather broad across the hips than thick and prominent behind, yet her backside looked handsome.—In fact she was straight and well shaped from top to toe, but if anything might have had broader shoulders with advantage, to make her proportionate to her height; yet only a sharp critic would have noticed that deficiency.

Her cunt, that important part of a woman, was large, but tight, fleshy inside, and muscular. It clipped my prick as deliciously as if it had been a much smaller one, and it was so healthy and deep, that often as I tried, I never could touch the orifice to her womb, either with my prick or my fingers. Nearly black hair, crisp and in full quantity was on her mons, and down the lips, and almost to her arsehole, but not round that brown orifice. The lips were thick and full, yet if she put her legs apart, they widened at once, showing deep crimson facings, and when shut a thin crimson streak.—Her nymphae were small.

She had dark brown, bright eyes, dark hair and good teeth—but her nose had been broken. That spoiled her face which otherwise would have been very handsome. As it was it did not make her ugly, but decidedly spoiled her.

She had the longest tongue I ever saw. She could put it further out of her mouth altogether than any one whom I have seen do that trick.—She was somewhat an unusual woman in every respect, and was I think twenty-four years old when I first saw her.—She had been a ballet dancer at some time, altho I only found that out after I had known her some months.—Her name was Sarah F**z**r.

She laid on the side of the bed, pulled her cunt open, knelt on the bed backside towards me, shewing cunt and arsehole together in quick succession as I asked her, and without uttering a word, but simply smiling as she obeyed. It had the usual effect,—a stiff-stander of the first order. It always is so with me. Objections, and sham modesty, a refusal to let me touch, and feel, or see, instead of whetting my appetite for a gay woman, always angers me and makes me lose desire.—With a woman not gay the case is different. The next minute I was enjoying her with impatience, then I lay on her stiff still, and full up her when I had spent.—'I shall do you again.' 'All right,' she replied. My prick never uncunted, but whilst reviving, my hands roved in all directions. She moved first this leg, then that, lifted her backside up, and seemed by instinct to know where my hands wished to go, and they were restless enough.—She was like Camille.—To something I said, she remarked.—'You're fond of it.'—As I recommenced my thrusts she said.—'Don't hurry, I want it,'—and we both spent together.—I forgot to mention that her flesh was of surprising firmness, and her backside solid and smooth.—I gave her the half sovereign as agreed—she did not ask for more, and we parted—but not for long.

The readiness with which she complied with all my wishes, together with the recollection of her personal charms, and the pleasure of her cunt, dwelt in my mind. I had her next night, and the night after, and then began to see her once or twice a week, and to indulge in voluptuous freaks which I had not done for three years or more, and which my imagination increased in its powers by what I had seen, read, and done, supplied me . . .

I went to the house first. Sarah entered followed by a very tall woman with her veil down, who stood and looked through it at me. Sarah having locked the door said, 'Take off your bonnet, Eliza.'—The woman only looked curiously round the room.—'Take off your bonnet.'—Then she took the bonnet off, and stood looking at me.—'Sit down,' said Sarah—and down she sat.

She was full thirty-five years old, but what a lovely creature.—I think I see her now, altho I never saw her but that once.—She had beautiful blue eyes, the lightest auburn hair crimped over her forehead, a beautiful pink bloom on her cheeks, and flesh quite white.—She was dressed in black silk, which contrasted well with her pink and white face.—She was big all over.—Big breasts jutted out in front—the tight sleeve shewed a big round arm—her ample bum filled the chair.—She was exactly what I wanted.—I never could wait long to talk with a woman whom I liked the look of, without proceeding to see, if not to feel, some of her hidden charms.—A burning desire to see what she had hidden seized me. I don't know if I spoke or not, but filled with desire, dropped on my knees and put my hand up her clothes, one round her thighs towards her bum, one towards her cunt.

As I touched her thighs, she put both hands down to stop me with a suppressed 'oh'—neither action or word, those of a woman who was shamming.—It wasn't the fierceness of a girl who first feels a man's hand about her privates, nor the sham modesty of a half-gay woman. It was the exclamation and manner of a woman not accustomed to strange hands about her privates. The next instant, I had reached both haunch and cunt.—She gave another start, my arms had lifted her petticoats, and I saw a big pair of legs in white stockings, and the slightest flesh above the knee nearly as white.—I placed my lips on it and kissed it—my hand slipped from her cunt round to her bum, and both hands now clasped one of the largest, and smoothest, and whitest backsides I ever felt. Then burrowing with my head under her petticoats, I kissed my way up her thighs till my nose touched her motte, and there I kept on kissing.

The warm close smell of her sweet flesh, mingled just with the faintest odour of cunt, rendered it impossible to keep my lips there long. The desire to enjoy her fully was unbearable—I withdrew my head and hands, and got up saying. 'Oh!—undress dear, I long to fuck you.'—They were the first words I had spoken to her, and she had not spoken at all.—She then rose up, and slowly began unbuttoning looking at Sarah.—'Lord, what a hurry you are in,' said Sarah to me.

Off went the black silk dress, out flashed two great but beautiful breasts over the top of the stays—and a pair of large, beautifully white arms shewed.—Then I saw the size of the big bum plainly under the petticoats. Off went stays and petticoats all but one.—Then she, '*There*, will that do?'

I wanted all off.—'Oh—I cannot take off any more.' I appealed to Sarah, who said. 'Now don't be a fool, Eliza'—Eliza then undressed to her chemise, and positively declared she would keep that on—I had taken off my trowsers and was standing cock in hand.—My impatience to discharge my seed into the splendid creature before me, made me careless whether she stripped or not.—I had drawn near to her—was feeling all round her bum with one hand, and wetting the fingers of the other in her cunt. I placed my prick so that it rubbed against her thigh, and feeling her, was at the same time pushing her towards the bed.

When we touched the bed—'I can't with Sarah there,' said the woman.—'Go out,' said I to Sarah. She looked savagely and replied, 'Nonsense.' Then I had a moment's dalliance and no more, forget what more was said or what took place, but saw Eliza on the bed, threw up her chemise, saw a mass of white flesh and a thicket of light hair between a pair of thighs, the next instant was between them, and my prick was up her cunt.

It was an affair of half a dozen shoves, a wriggle, a gush, and I had enjoyed her. Then I became tranquil enough to think of the woman, in whose vagina I had taken my pleasure. Resting on one arm and feeling her all over with one hand, I looked at her, and she at me. I said a few endearing words, as she lay tranquilly with my cock still stiff and up her.

I could have done it again right off, but had not yet looked at her hidden charms, and desire to inspect her quim made me draw out my cock and rise on my knees between her legs. Few strange women like their cunt looked at, when sperm is running out of it. She pushed down her chemise, I got off her, and then without saying a word she washed. When I had washed my cock it was as stiff as ever. I went to the side of the bed where she had just begun piddling, and held my stiff one in front of her eyes. For the first time she smiled.

She began to dress, but I told her I had only begun my amusement. I had brought bottles of champagne, for I knew how that liquor opens the hearts and the legs of women.—We got glasses and began drinking.—She drank it well and soon began to talk and laugh. When I again brought her to the bed she was an altered woman, but still did not seem to like fucking before Sarah. 'Why I have seen all you have got to show often enough,' said Sarah angrily.—On the bed now for a good look at the cunt.—It was a big one.—An inch of fat at least covered the split, stoutish middle-aged women get I think fat cunt lips, and hers was very large.—She had a very strongly developed clitoris, and such a lot of light hair. Large and fat as the cunt was, I do not recollect if the prick hole was large or little but know that I enjoyed her as much as a man possibly could. I delighted in laying my hand between two, long, fat cunt lips—I rolled over her, played with and kissed her from her thighs to her eyes, frigged her clitoris till she wriggled, and as at length my prick slipped up her cunt again, she whispered, 'What a devil you are.' She pushed her tongue out, mine met it, and then all was over.—She wagged her big arse vigorously when spending.

Ballocks and cunt again cleared of sperm, to the champagne we again went.—Sarah had not yet undressed, I had almost forgotten her. Now I made her strip, and my two big women were nearly naked together.—A little more pfiz and we were all on the spree.—Eliza still had the manner of a woman not accustomed to expose her charms, but insisted on by me and Sarah who seemed to have control over her,

off went her chemise at last.—Off went my shirt—and
there we all stood naked.

I never before had two such big women together
and did with them all that my baudy fancy
prompted.—I put them belly to belly, then bum to
bum.—Then standing up before the glass. I put my
prick between their two bums, making them squeeze
it between their buttocks whilst I groped both cunts,
and frigged at once both of them. Then putting Eliza
at the side of the bed with open thighs, I put Sarah
between them as if she were a man—and pushing my
prick between her thighs just touched her split.—She
laid hold of my prick and slipped it up her own
cunt.—But I did not mean that, and pulled it
out.—Then I had them both side by side on the bed,
and scarcely knew which of the gaping cunts to put
into, but the fair haired one again had my attention.
Then I put Sarah upside down on the bed so that her
arse and cunt were near the pillow, one leg partly
doubled up, and one cocked up against the back of
the bed, and looking at her thus I fucked Eliza by her
side. Sarah said she must frig herself and set to work
doing it, whilst with the one hand stretched back she
played round my prick stem in Eliza's cunt which
was tightening under the pleasure of my shoving and
probing. Eliza's amativeness had been awakened, she
clasped me tightly with her large white arms, kissed
and thrust her tongue into my mouth, in a state of
the fullest voluptuous enjoyment.

We finished the champagne and sent out for sand-
wiches, stout, and brandy.—I had taken the room for
the night.—Sarah never was, and her companion was
not in a hurry now. We ate, drank, and got more
erotic.—Eliza's fat bum was on my naked thighs. She

put her hand on my prick, and grasping it for a minute whispered, 'Come and do it again.'—Sarah said, 'What are you whispering about?'—She had been looking at times annoyed at my taking no notice of her.—Again I put Eliza on the bed.—Sarah who had alternately been quiet and then baudy, said, 'It's my turn, why don't you poke me?'—'You will have it another night.'—She then got on to the bed, and on to the top of Eliza, kissed her rapturously, got between her thighs, and my two big beauties were like man and woman in each other's arms.—Eliza threw up her legs until her heels were on Sarah's back. Sarah nestling her belly close up to her, the hair of their two cunts intermingled.—Sarah's arse wriggled in a quiet way. 'Don't now —don't'—said the other—Sarah took no heed, wriggled on, then lay quiet, and after a time rolled gently off Eliza, left the bed, and sat down in the arm chair.—I looked at her very white face. 'You've spent,' I said—she laughed.

I fucked Eliza then, and laying with prick in her asked her in a whisper to meet me again. 'I cannot, I dare not,' said she.—I could not get out of her her name, or where to find her again.

Eliza was now half screwed. No sooner had I fucked her than she began squeezing my prick.—She opened her large thighs, placed my finger on her clitoris, kissed my prick, thrust her tongue in my mouth, and did every thing which a randy-arsed woman does to get more fucking.—I fucked her four or five times, perhaps more, and till neither she nor Sarah could make my cock stand. The house was closed, off I went, but not until Eliza had gone long.—Sarah insisted on that.—Then said Sarah, 'I'm not going without a poke.' With infinite trouble she got a fuck out of me, and both of us groggy, we separated.

Some nights after talking of Eliza, whose legs in boots and silk stockings had charmed me, Sarah laughed.—'Why, they were mine, I lent them to her.' Then I recollected that Sarah had not had her usual boots on.

I wished her to get me Eliza again. She refused. I said I would find her out.—She was sure I should not!—I went to one or two places on the chance of finding her, and Sarah laughed when I told her.—I used to get awfully randy when I thought of the two big women naked together. 'She is not gay, altho you may think so, it was only because she was so dreadfully hard up that she came,' Sarah averred.

'If she wasn't gay, she did all I asked her.' 'As she was getting screwed, and I had told her what you expected her to do.' 'And she spent like fun after the first time.' 'Oh yes I saw, and I told her about it afterwards.' 'Where did she go that night?' 'To my lodgings and slept with me.' 'If you don't bring her, I won't see you any more,'—and for a fortnight I did not—I used to go up to her in the street and ask her. She said she couldn't even if she would.—'You are lucky to have had her at all.' 'I paid handsomely.' 'If you hadn't you would never have had her.'—I expect that now and then married women make a bit of money by their cunts.

Then things went on as before, but as I pulled Sarah's cunt about, I used to compare it with Eliza's.—Sarah seemed to me to know Eliza's cunt as well as if it had been her own.

Just then Sarah met the man with the donkey prick,

whom she told me did then exactly what he had done before with her. This recital made me wild with desire.—I told her I would give her something handsome, if she could find a house, where I could see couples fucking. She had heard there was one, but those who knew would not tell, and some time slipped away.—With a smiling face one night she said, 'If you don't mind a sovereign for the room, and five shillings afterwards for each couple you see, I know now where you can get what you want.'—Off we went the following night to the house, and through a carefully prepared hole beneath a picture frame, I had a complete view of a nice room.—The washing place, bed (no sofa), looking-glass, fire place, were all in sight. In fact only that side of the room in which the eye hole was made in the partition, was not perfectly visible.

I recollect that first night well.—The woman of the house said to me, 'You won't tell people will you?'—Then—'Put out your light when you are looking.'—There was gas in the room.—'Don't make a noise—and don't look till you hear, or think they are on the bed.'—Then she lifted a picture up on to a higher nail in the partition, which disclosed a small hole.—Then she went into the other room, and did the same to a picture there. It was in a huge, old fashioned, projecting gilt frame, which when hung higher up, just cleared the hole but well shadowed it.—There was one good, strong, gas burner in the room, but no candle to enable people to pry about with.

The hole was so high up, that it was necessary to stand on a sofa placed just against the partition. There was no fire in our room when first I went there, and it was dark at about seven o'clock, Sarah had gone in first.—The woman when she had got my sovereign said, 'I don't suppose any one will be there till about eight o'clock.'

I undressed Sarah, and sat in excitement feeling her about, and looking at her legs, and talking.—I heard couples going into lower rooms, and the woman saying, 'This way, sir'—a gruff voice reply,—'I won't go so high.'—At length a couple entered. Sarah turned down the gas in our room, and up I got on the sofa. Oh my delight—how I wish it were to come over again. There was a fine young man and a niceish young woman—I watched them with an intensity of lust quite indescribable.—I saw him first pay her, she take off her things, piss, and then stand naked expectantly. He took off his trowsers, she took hold of his prick, and he felt her cunt.—Then it was kiss, feel, and frig on both sides. I could hear him ask questions, and she reply. Then he put her down on a chair, and pushed his noble prick up against her but not up her. Then he brought her to the side of the bed. I saw her thighs distended, a dark haired cunt opened and looked at. He pushed his prick up it and had a plunge or two. (His back was towards me then.) Apparently not satisfied, he then pushed her straight on the bed—got on himself, laid by the side of her, and then I saw his prick in all its glory.—She wanted to handle it, he would not let her, but fingered her cunt with his hand nearest to her.

At length kneeling between her thighs I saw it again in all its prominence, stiff and nodding—until dropping on to her belly, it was hidden from my sight.—I watched the heavings and thrustings—the saucers which came in his arse cheeks, and disappeared as he

245

thrust up and withdrew his penis, her thighs move up, and then her legs cross over his, as she heaved to meet his strokes.—Then the shoves became mere wriggles, then were loud exclamations of pleasure, then all was still. His limbs stretched out, her legs came tranquilly down to the side of his, a long kiss or two was heard, then absolute silence.—It was a delicious sight.

Almost before he had finished, I had put the cork in the hole in the partition, pulled Sarah to the side of the bed, felt her cunt, and was about to put up it, when alas I spent all over her outside, on thighs and cunt, then with my cock still dripping I got on the sofa again.—Sarah with me, for she seemed to enjoy looking as much as I did.

He had risen on to his knees between her thighs, and held his prick in his right hand, I could just see its red tip.—'Don't move, I'll fuck you again.' 'Well, you must give me some more.' 'I will give you five shillings.' 'Very well, shall I wash?' 'No stay as you are.'—Slowly his bum sunk on to his heels—his head peered forward—his left hand went to her cunt.—'My spunk's running out,' he said. 'Oh you beast.' He flopped down on her without another word—and I saw by the action of his buttocks that he was driving his pego up her.—His hands clasped her again, I saw the saucers in his arse—his short shoves—her wriggles and jerks—and heard her sighs and 'oha's.' Then soon his silence shewed that his pleasure was complete.

During all this I kept telling Sarah in a whisper what I saw—she got as impatient as me and wanted to see as much.—It often was, 'Let me have a look.' 'I shan't.' 'What is she doing?'

'She is doing so and so,'—then I let her peep and

she would tell *me*.—I sat on the sofa whilst she was standing and looking, grasped her arse, put my lips on her cunt, and pulled her towards me, giving utterance to all sorts of baudy extravagances in whispers.—It is odd it occurs to me, that all *she* wanted to see was what the *woman* was doing—what *I* principally wanted to see was what the *man* was doing.—At all times that I was at that peep hole, the same feelings were predominant in both of us.

The man was pleased, gave the extra money, told her he would meet her again, washed his prick and went off—she leisurely washed her cunt, and off she went—then lighting the gas, I ballocked Sarah—not letting my sperm be wasted outside this time.—'It's exciting,' said she, 'I have not seen such a thing since the night you had the fine, tall, fair woman—and it makes me as randy as be damned' (her favourite expression). We finished fucking just in time for another couple. We saw three couples the first night.

I am not going to tell all I saw—much of it was common-place fucking enough—yet some had the charm of novelty, and altho I was there perhaps in the course of a year or two, in all fifty or sixty times, and saw nearly a hundred and fifty couples fucking, never grew tired of seeing.

The most amusing thing to me was that Sarah wanted to see so much.—After a time I put her occasionally with her back against the partition, and my prick up her—and then applying my eye to the hole over her shoulder, fucked her, and looked at the fucking couple in the room, until I lost sight of them, in the excitement of my own physical pleasure.

That was a risky thing to do for they could have heard us, as well as we did them. But usually the couples were so absorbed by lewedness, so preoccupied by fucking or anticipation of it, that they rarely seemed to notice anything.

Two or three weeks after I had used this peep hole, Sarah said she had again met the man with the titanic prick.—We had by that time got so intimate, that she told me any funny adventures she had with men.—He had behaved in just the same manner to her, and was to meet her that day week.—'Oh! I long to see him with you—bring him to the next room,'—and it was so arranged.—The spying room was to be kept for me—the back room I was to pay a pound for, and it was to be kept for Sarah. The old baud knew what we were up to.—I told Sarah to keep the man as long as she could, whether he paid much or little (he gave her treble what I did), and above all to manage so that I could see his prick well.

The evening came, I was there before the time, and thought that they were never coming.—At length I saw them enter—I had been in a fever lest it should not come off.—The whole evening's spectacle is photographed on my brain.—I recollect almost every word that was said.—What I did not hear, Sarah told me afterwards, tho that was but little.

'Take off your things,' said he.—Sarah undressed to her chemise.—His back was towards me, his hand was evidently on his prick.—'Ain't you going to take *your* clothes off, you had better—you can do it nicer.'—He evidently had not intended that, but yielded to her suggestion.—When in his shirt he went up to her, she gradually turned round so that *her* back and *his* face were towards me, and her movement was so natural that no one could have guessed her object, altho I did.—Moving then slightly on one side, she put her hands to his shirt, lifted the tail, and out stood the largest prick I ever saw. 'Oh what a giant you've got,' said she.—He laughed loudly.—'Is it not, did you ever see a bigger?' 'No, but your balls are not so big.' 'No, but they are *big*.' 'No,' she said. 'You can't see them,'—and he put one leg on a chair,—Sarah stooped and looked under them.—Whilst doing so, he tried to give her a whack on her head with his prick—and laughed loudly at his own fun.—'Why,' said Sarah, 'if your balls were equal in size to your prick, you wouldn't be able to get them into your trousers.'—He laughed loudly, saying, 'They're big enough—there is plenty of spunk in them.'

Sarah went on admiring it, smoothing it with her hand, pulling up and down the foreskin and keeping it just so that I had a full view. 'You are hairy,' said she, rubbing his thigh.—Then I noticed he was hairy on his legs, which was very ugly.—'Yes, do you like hairy-skinned men?' 'I hate a man smooth like a woman—take off your shirt and let me see.' 'It's cold.' 'Come close to the fire then.'—She talked quite loudly purposely, tho it was scarcely needed. His voice was a clear and powerful one.—Without seeming anxious about it, but flattering him, she managed to get his shirt off and he stood naked.—He was a tall man, very well-built, and hairy generally. Masses hung from his breasts, it darkened his arms. It peeped out like beards from his armpits, it spread from his balls half way up his belly, he had a dark beard, and thick black hair.—In brief he was a big, powerful, hairy, ugly fellow, but evidently very proud of his prick, and all belonging to him. Her flattering remarks evidently pleased him highly, and he turned round as she wished him, to let her see him well all over.—His prick which had been stiff had fallen down, for instead of thinking of the woman, he was now thinking of himself; but it was when hanging, I should say, six inches long, and thick in proportion. 'Dam it, it's cold, we are not so accustomed to strip like you women.'—Then he put his shirt on and began business.

He made her strip and told her to go to the bedside. She went to the end and leaned over it with backside towards him.—He tucked his shirt well up, came behind her, and with his prick which had now stiffened and seemed nine inches long (I really think longer), hit her over her buttocks as if with a stick. It made a spanking noise as it came against her flesh. Then he shoved it between her thighs, brought it out again, and went on thwacking her buttocks with it.—'Don't it hurt you?' she asked him turning her head round towards the peep hole.—'Look here,' said he. Going to a round small mahogany table and taking the cloth off it—he thwacked, and banged his prick on it, and a sound came as if the table had been hit with a stick.—'It does not hurt me,' he said.—I never was so astonished in my life.

'I mean to fuck you,' said he. 'That you shan't, you will hurt any woman.'—Again he roared with laughter.—'Suck it.' 'I shan't.'—Again he laughed.— Then he made her lean on a chair, and again banged his prick against her arse.—Then he sat down, and pulled her on to him, so that his prick came up between her thighs just in front of her quim.—'I wish there was a big looking-glass,' said he. 'Why did you come here, there was one at the other house.'—Sarah said this was nicer and cleaner, and he had said he wanted a quiet house.—'Ah, but I shan't come here again, I don't like the house.'

'Get on to the chairs—the same as before.' But the chairs in the room were very slight, and Sarah was frightened of them slipping away from under her.—So she placed one chair against the end of the bed, and steadied it; and against another which she put a slight distance off, she pushed the large table. Then mounting on the chairs, she squatted with one foot on each as if pissing. I could not very well see her cunt for her backside was towards me, and shadowed it.

He laid down with his head between the chairs, and just under her cunt. He had taken the bolster and pillows from the bed for his head, and there he laid looking up at her gaping slit, gently frigging his prick all the time. At length he raised himself on one hand, and licked away at her cunt for several minutes, his big prick throbbing, and knocking up against his belly whilst he did it.

Said he again, 'I wish there was a glass,' Sarah got down, and put on the floor the small glass of the dressing table, and arranged it so that he could see a little of himself as he lay.—But he was not satisfied.—He recommended cunt-licking, and self-frigging, and all was quiet for a minute.—Then he actually roared out, —'Oh—my spunk coming, my spunk,—my spunk,—spunk—oho.—Come down—come over me.'—Off got Sarah, pushed away the chairs, stood over him with legs distended, her arse towards me so that I lost sight of his face, but could see his legs, belly, and cock as he lay on the floor.—'Stoop,—lower,—lower-'—She half squatted, he frigged away, her cunt was now within about six inches of his prick, when frigging hard and shouting out quite loudly—'Hou—Hou—Hou,' his sperm shot out right on to her cunt or thereabouts, and he went on frigging till his prick lessening, he let it go, and flop over his balls.

Sarah washed her cunt and thighs, and turning round before doing so, stood facing me and pointed to her cunt. His spunk lay thick on the black hair tho I could barely see it.—She smiled and turned away. He lay still on the floor with eyes closed for full five minutes, as if sleep. Sarah washed, put on her chemise and sat down by the fire, her back towards me partly.

He came to himself, got up and went to the fire—then he washed (his back towards me), then stood by the fire, then fetched the pot and pissed. I saw his great flabby tool in his hand, and the stream sparkling out of it, for it was done just under the gas light.—Again he stood by the fire, his tool hidden by his shirt which he had on, and they talked.—Then he strode round the room and looked at the prints on the wall, looked even at the very picture beneath which I was peeping.—'What a daub,' he remarked and passed on (it was a miserable portrait of a man), then from the pocket of his trousers he gave Sarah several sovereigns.

That lady knew her game, and had thrown up her chemise so as to warm her thighs—and after he had paid her, he put his hand on to them.—She at the same time put her hand on to his tool. 'Oh what a big one.'—nothing evidently pleased him so much as talking about the size.—'Did you ever see so big an one,' said he for the sixth time I think. 'Never—let's look at it well.—Hold up your shirt.'—He did as told.—Sarah pulled his prick up, then let it fall, handled his balls, pulled the foreskin up and down, and shewed him off again for my advantage.—'Why don't you sit down, are you in a hurry?' Down he sat, his tool was becoming thicker and longer under her clever handling, and hung down over the edge of the chair. He was sitting directly under the gas light, and I could see plainly, for Sarah cunningly had even stirred the fire into a blaze. He was curious about other men's cocks—what their length and thickness was.—She shewed him by measuring on his own, and kept pulling it about, her object being to get it stiff again for me to see his performances.—My delight was extreme—I could scarcely believe that I was actually seeing what I did, and began to wish to feel his prick myself. How large it must feel in the hand I thought, how small mine is compared with it, and I felt my own.—As Sarah pulled down his prepuce, I involuntarily did so to mine, and began to wish she were feeling mine instead of the man's.

Then only I noticed how white his prick was. His flesh was brownish—and being so sprinkled with hair it made it look dark generally.—His prick looked quite white by contrast. Sarah must have been inspired that night, for no woman could have better used her opportunity for giving me pleasure and instruction. Repeating her wonder at the size, she said, 'Let's see how it looks when you kneel.'—He actually knelt as she desired. I saw his prick hanging down between his legs. Soon after in another attitude, I noticed that hair crept up between his bum cheeks, and came almost into tufts on to the cheeks themselves.—I saw that his prick was now swelling.—Sarah taking hold of it, 'Why it's stiff again.' He grasped it in the way

I had first seen him, and said eagerly.—'Let's see your cunt again.'

Sarah half slewed her chair round towards him, opened both legs wide, and put up one of her feet against the mantelpiece, as I have often seen her do when with me. He knelt down and I lost sight of his head between her legs—but saw his hand gently frigging himself as before, and heard soon a splashy, sloppy, slobbery sort of suck, as his tongue rubbed on her cunt now wetted by his saliva. Then he got up and pushed his prick against her face.—'Suck, and I will give you another sovereign.' 'It will choke me—I won't,' said Sarah.

Then he began to rub her legs and said he liked silk stockings, that few wore silk excepting French women whom he did not like,—but 'they all suck my prick.'—Again Sarah put up her leg—again he licked her cunt, and then said she must frig him, which she agreed to on his paying another sovereign.

He told her to go to the edge of the bed and he then went to the side nearest the door, which put his back towards me.—He called her there.—'Come here,' said Sarah, laying herself down at the foot. 'No, here.' 'I won't, it's cold close to the door' (she knew that there I could not see his cock). He obeyed, put up her legs (just as I used to do) opened them wide, and I could sideways see her black haired quim gaping. 'Close them,' he cried. She did and lay on her back, her knees and heels together up to her bum, 'I'll spend over your silk stockings,' said he, now frigging violently. Sarah to save her stockings, just as his spunk spurted, opened her legs wide and it went over her cunt and belly.—He never seemed to notice it.

I had passed an intensely exciting couple of hours by myself, watching this man with his huge fucking machine. Sarah in her attitudes, altho I had seen them fifty times, looked more inviting than ever. My prick had been standing on and off for an hour.—I would have fucked anything in the shape of cunt if it had been in hand, and nearly groaned for want of one. As I saw her legs open to receive his squirt, heard his shout of pleasure, and saw his violent, frig, frig, frig, I could restrain myself no longer, but giving my cock a few rubs, spent against the partition, keeping my eye at the peephole all the while.

He wiped his cock on her cunt hair, washed, and went away seemingly in a hurry.—Sarah came in to me.—'Don't you want me,' said she.—I pointed to my spunk on the partition. 'You naughty boy, I want it awfully.'—Soon after I was fucking her.—With all her care to save her silk stockings, sperm had hit her calf, and while I fucked her at the bed side, I made her hold up her leg that I might look at it.—It excited me awfully. What a strange thing lust is.

NEXUS NEW BOOKS

To be published in March

WHIPPING BOY
G. C. Scott
£5.99

Richard and his German girlfriend Helena have cocooned themselves in the English countryside, to live out their private – and elaborate – fantasies of submission and domination. But their rural idyll is threatened by the arrival of Helena's aunt Margaret – an imperious woman with very strict house rules and some very shady friends, who always gets what she wants. And what she wants is Richard . . .

ISBN 0 352 33595 5

ACCIDENTS WILL HAPPEN
Lucy Golden
£5.99

Julie Markham embarks on a game whose rules she does not know, and in just three short days her life is turned upside-down. On Friday she was happily engaged to be married. By Monday, she is crouching naked on a cold floor and suffering whatever any man or woman demands. The two days in between have been a very wet weekend – and the best of her life.

ISBN 0 352 33596 3

EROTICON 3
Ed. J-P Spencer
£5.99

Like its predecessors in the series, this volume contains a dozen extracts from once-forbidden erotic texts – from the harems of the Pashas (*A Night in a Moorish Harem*) to the not-so-chaste devotions of a French nunnery (*The Pleasures of Lolotte*).

ISBN 0 352 33597 1